DEATH ENGINE
PROTOCOL
Better Dying Through Science

I0662458

Margret A. Treiber

Azoth Khem Publishing
Huntsville, AL
April 2025

AZOTH KHEM

ISBN: 978-1-952880-23-0

For permission queries, contact Azoth Khem Publishing:
Nancy Chandler
AzothKhemPublishing@gmail.com

Printed in the United States of America

Dedication

This book is dedicated to all my fellow tweaks out there. Don't let the fucktards bring you down. Let your inner rage give them hell.

Contents

Part 1: Beginning is easy; continuing is shit. 1

Chapter 1 1

Chapter 2 23

Chapter 3 40

Chapter 4 67

Chapter 5 97

Part 2: The Road To Hell Is Paved With Shit. 124

Chapter 6 124

Chapter 7 144

Chapter 8 164

Part 3: An ounce of discretion is worth a pound of shit.
.... 178

Chapter 9 178

Chapter 10 197

Chapter 11 222

Part 1: Beginning is easy; continuing is shit.

Chapter 1

Another concussive blast connected with my head, audibly fracturing my elderly skull. Suddenly, I was in the air, weightless and free. Then, just as abruptly, there was a wall—a substantial wall and a fuckton of pain. My neck crunched as it jammed up into my cranium.

I tried to laugh at my assailant and tell him his attack was as meaningless as his fucktastic life. Instead, all that came out was, "The palmetto bells watusi da da da down wub," followed by a stream of vomit.

Great. Freaking brain damage.

The cognitive impairment itself wasn't particularly painful; just verbally inconvenient. I gazed up at the hazy visage of RoboBash's metallic face shield. It should have been smooth, with a mirrored finish. Instead, it warped into a lumpy mass, slowly melting from my vision until there was nothing but blackness.

Now, my pain was coming.

At first, there was nothing. Only darkness accompanied me. Then, the heavens expanded into my reality. It blossomed from a single blue-green dot into a perfect tropical seashore.

The ocean waves caressed my toes as the sun warmed my tired bones. A breeze brushed my cheek as I opened my eyes and gazed upon the flawless paradise. Yawning the clean, fresh breeze into my lungs, I sat up and enjoyed the moment's tranquility. It had been so long.

A pang of grief struck me as my cognitive faculties started to return. I had been enjoying a perfectly clear night in my backyard, downing gummies and chugging tea when out of the fucking blue Robodouche decided to bum-rush me in my lawn chair. He not only harshed my buzz, but killed me in the process. Why now? What the hell did that twat want?

"Fuck," I cursed. This was going to suck.

Things in my home at Champion Acres had been virtually serene, well, compared to my working days. Now it was about to become shit again.

Down the beach, a man waved at me from a distance. So familiar. I knew him but couldn't place him. It had been so long. He grinned and waved as a halo of late-afternoon sunlight bathed his body.

"Don't look at the light," I reminded myself. "Never look at the light."

But I did. I gazed upon its—his body, the light. The radiance of the blue sky contrasted with the warm, intense luminance. The fierce glow seduced my eyes. The blue faded to sapphire, then indigo, then oblivion. The man dissipated, partially absorbed by the brilliance. The rest of my tropical paradise joined the void of nothing. I tried to avert my eyes, but there was only the light. The incredible, spectacular light called to me, drawing me in, suffocating me. Tired of fighting, I let go, releasing myself to the universe's will. So peaceful, drifting, warm. So temporary.

CRACK

The glow shattered as RoboBash's left fist pulled back from his most recent skull-shattering blow.

"Moth…effin…light," I groaned.

"Ha, ha!" he mocked. "Puny old crone, maybe a little overrated. Now, I will send you into the light!"

My eye twitched open momentarily, just long enough to see RoboBash flex his body, wind up his final blow, and declare victory.

"Nobody can defeat me," he proclaimed to the cosmos.

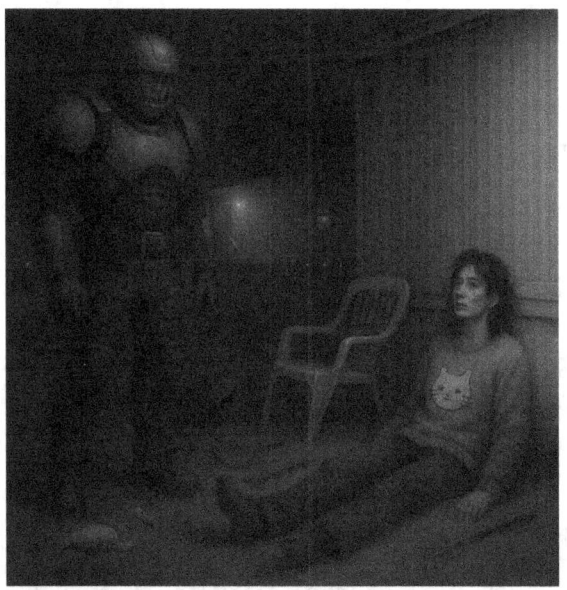

My body seized.

Robo laughed at what he perceived to be my final death throes. He was sorely incorrect. I was done dying. Worse than that, I was healing. And there was nothing anyone could do about it.

The process was anything but pleasant. Far from it. The sensation of bone knitting, flesh regenerating, and fierce antibodies doing a perfectly choreographed dance of 'fuck you' to my already angry nerve endings. Then, as if that wasn't enough, a new sensation of electro-hell compounded the agony. Millions of microscopic shocks coursed across my body.

Robo's right fist connected with the left side of my face just as an electric field swaddled me. His mech armor's robotic fist sprayed white-hot sparks. He yelled in surprise.

"What?"

"The light is a lie," I panted. "It only brings you back."

Robo snarled and examined his shorting appendage. "You were dead."

"Oh, yeah—that." I stood up, hearing my neck bones audibly snapping back into place as I moved. "Someone set you up, buddy. There's only one way to kill me, and nobody has the patience."

RoboBash shook his head. "I am not a patient man. You will die now. Again."

"See, this is what I'm talking about," I said, rolling my eyes in futility. "Just stop!"

Robo wound up for another frontal assault. His fist didn't have a chance to connect before he was struck by another sphincter-loosening surge of electricity. Apparently, I had acquired electrical abilities this time, and Robo needed to eat less cabbage.

Given the tremendous pain I was in, I executed the best saunter I could. I stood over RoboBash, acrid smoke billowing from his torso. He was clearly conscious, but would not move anytime soon. I reached into my pocket and pulled out a handful of crumpled cash coins. Dropping the money at Robo's feet, I taunted him.

"Here, buy yourself a surge protector." I staggered away. The acrid smell of electrified flesh almost overwhelmed the fresh floral scents of paradise that still lingered in my memory and teased my senses.

The media was quick to pounce and unkind to RoboBash. The community's security cameras recorded the entire event. Headlines like "Robo Bashed by Elderly!" and "Taking out the RoboTrash" spammed the internet. I felt a twinge of regret, but then again, I hadn't actually done anything but not stay dead.

I left the Acres in a hurry, with only the clothes on my back and my stash of cash coins. With no reason to lie low, I returned to the old neighborhood. It wasn't a long public transit ride, and I had the entire car to myself. Watching the featureless landscape through the window, I took advantage of the quiet, attempting to center myself and focus, but it wasn't working. My body chemistry was still jacked up from the regeneration—neurotransmitters scrambled, hormone levels erratic, and my nervous system firing like it was stuck in a perpetual panic loop. I felt like rampaging in a fit of destruction and then crawling under a rock and dying. Plus, the anxiety of the unknowns ricocheted through my traumatized mind. I couldn't find space in my head to retreat into. It was all chaos and triggers. Every motion my peripheral vision caught, every sound, every bump in the road ignited my neurons, pumping increasing volumes of adrenaline into my bloodstream. Peace eluded me. Why the attack? Why now? What would be my next move?

This time around, I thought I had figured it out. I dug in some place relatively local, some place no one would suspect. Everyone assumed I'd change continents or even go off-world after what happened. I knew that hiding nearby would throw them off. And it worked for a while, maybe even longer than I had a right to expect.

The transit terminal was surprisingly clean. It was modern and shiny—as if it had recently been remodeled. I looked around for anything familiar, a reminder of the old days, but there was only new. I was the relic, the twenty-something in old lady clothes who regenerated back to a state of optimal gene expression upon every violent death.

I ducked into a CheapTree. The place buzzed with substandard LED lighting and a faint antiseptic smell. I grabbed some generic pants, a couple of T-shirts, a backpack, and some basic toiletries. I paid and then changed in the store bathroom. I felt a pang of sadness as I discarded the torn, fuzzy pink cat sweater. My neighbor, Dori, had made it for me for my birthday.

Stepping out into the city, I was struck by the sounds of people. I took a moment to breathe in the activity. It did feel good to be back. The buildings remained as I remembered. The majority of the changes were in the people. There were fewer of them than I recalled. There was also a heaviness about them. The accessories, the clothing styles, the popular store chains, the posters, and the signs were all a little bleaker and emptier. The times had changed, even if the basic architecture had not.

When I went under, the cultural vibe was positive, bright, and optimistic. Now, I was stunned by contemporary culture's negativity and darkness. I had escaped it for some time, living in my sheltered community, enjoying blissful ignorance. At present, the media spoke of impending doom and the downfall of civilization as we knew it. Signs screamed slogans like "Vote with Your Coin. Don't buy Earth Goods" and "Life on Earth Equals Death."

It was somewhat of a downer.

"Eris," a male voice called from behind me. "Is that you?"

"Depends." An electric spark shot from my finger and snapped to the concrete sidewalk as I spun around. "Who's asking?"

"It's me." The man pointed at his chest. "Tyler."

"Tyler!" I studied the lines on his face and his graying hair. "Wow, last time I saw you, you were like—"

"Twenty-two," Tyler interjected. "I was a Junior Legionnaire."

I remembered the Junior Legionnaire PR fiasco. Although Tyler had been inspired by the internship, several fourteen-year-old girls had entirely different experiences. I caught Major Everything more than a few times, giving personalized training to the teens, even after our marriage.

"Yeah," I nodded. "It was a while ago. So, what are you up to now?"

"Oh." Tyler shrugged and looked down at the sidewalk. "I'm out of the business. I'm in insurance now."

"Insurance." I laughed. "Shit, there has to be a joke in there somewhere."

Tyler grinned. "Yeah, I suppose there should be."

"Yup." I shifted uncomfortably, searching my mind for a suitable response.

"So, I saw what happened with RoboBash the other day. Sorry."

"Yeah, that was unfortunate." My eye twitched with the memory.

"How long did you make it this time?"

"About thirty-three years. It's not the longest, but close. They always suck me back in."

"Who? The Nod, People Prime?"

"Don't know," I shrugged. "Could be a new player this time. You never know."

"True." Tyler looked down again and sighed. "Does it still hurt bad, like it used to? Did it get better with time, like you hoped?"

I shook my head. "No, the pain still sucks like donkey dong."

Tyler laughed this time. "Sorry…"

"Ah… no, it's cool. I can't get used to it, but I can have a sense of humor about it."

"So," he motioned to the black mark my spark left on the sidewalk. "Electric stuff this time?"

"Ayup," I replied. "I feel all tingly now."

"Well, try not to destroy the power grid."

I grinned. "I'll consider your suggestion."

"See you around?" Tyler asked. "I still pop into Spaz sometimes."

"It's still there? Al still running it?"

"Al still owns and runs the place."

"Maybe I'll check it out."

"Cool." Tyler waved. "See you later, then."

I watched him walk off and tried to calculate the years. What happened when? How did it get so complicated? My recent brain injury wasn't helping my memory.

Spaz was a unique place. The locale itself wasn't strange. In essence, it was just a dive bar that sold food. It was the clientele that made it different. Some called it a tweak bar. It was populated by the genetically modified, the engineered, and people who wished they were one of the two. It didn't matter if you were good, bad, or indifferent. The only prerequisite seemed to be that you had a corporeal form and worked in the business. Although management frowned upon physical confrontation within the premises, this did not stop the more-than-occasional brawl.

As I stepped inside, I was struck by how little the place had changed in my absence. The furniture, lighting, and pictures on the wall were all like stepping into the past. Even the row of slot machines lining the back wall was precisely as I remembered. The only difference was a new picture above the machines: a smiling, elderly Asian man.

I walked up to the bar, ordered a beer, sat in a back booth, and leisurely sipped. People buzzed around the place, drinking, venting, cutting deals, but the crowd was thinner than I recalled. I recognized a few faces: Sam the Fixer, George, and Tye the Henchman for hire, among others. Although these bastards were older, time had not changed their basic shticks. You could see how each was well-established, but like everything else I had witnessed in this modern fucktopia, their façade was weak. These posers were all trying to look heroic, dangerous, fiendish—whatever their thing was—but they were stale. They were dry, day-old toast served with synthetic butter on my genetically altered breakfast table—a tasteless bite of nostalgia that promised flavor but delivered disappointment. I had already tasted the meal they promised, and it was bland.

I turned my attention to what had the potential for a minor scuffle. One dude was taunting another about a disastrous defeat, and the other guy was already drunk and belligerent. It had the makings of an early evening's entertainment.

The one guy got in the other's face, shouting something raucous about his mother. The second dude turned purple with rage and shoved him. In response, the first idiot swung his arm back for a telegraphed roundhouse punch. Just as his fist fully wound up—before he could strike—a large hand reached over and stopped him. It belonged to the owner, Al.

"You need to leave," Al's deep, mechanical voice bellowed.

"Fuck off, robot." The guy started to square up to Al.

"You need to leave," Al repeated without flinching. "Now. Before I hurt you."

The guy looked into Al's tarnished metal face and backed down.

"Thought so," Al said. He pointed at the other guy. "You need to leave, too."

The other guy started to speak but thought better of it. He grabbed his coat and left.

"That was very butch of you." I winked at Al.

He caught my glance and spun around. "There is a certain expectation of aggression I must maintain."

"It's a good thing they don't know that you don't know how to fight," I whispered.

"I know how to fight." Al pulled a heavy metal chair from a low stack along the wall and sat across from me. "I choose not to."

"Yeah, yeah—that's what you say, but I never see any evidence to back it up."

Al shook his head.

"You know I was enjoying that little spat. I was rooting for the drunk guy."

"They were both drunk," Al replied.

"Details," I smirked.

"Sorry for ruining your entertainment, Eris. Have to keep repair costs down."

"I guess I can forgive you… this time."

"It's good to see you." He reached out to shake my hand. I pulled my arm back.

"Not safe. I have some kind of electricity thing going on this time."

Al nodded. "I saw the news feed."

"Yeah. Any freak with a thick enough wallet can buy body armor and pretend to be a robot nowadays."

"Yes, it seems that way. Have you slept yet?"

I shrugged. "I'll get a room later. I'm okay."

"You're a bad liar," Al said. "I can see it in your face."

"Yeah, and speaking of faces… I see you're showing yours now. Did you finally come out of the mainframe?"

Al shook his head. "I was severely injured in combat and rebuilt with industrial parts."

"Ah, that's the spin," I smirked and leaned toward Al, resting my elbows on the table. "And people buy it?"

"Why wouldn't they?" Al shifted forward, his face just inches from mine. "They have no reason to question it."

We stared awkwardly at each other until I broke eye contact and took a sip of beer. "Heard about Ji-hoon a while back. Sorry. I didn't know him well. He seemed like a nice old man."

Al made a noise that sounded like an attempt at a laugh. "Ji-hoon was never a nice old man. He had a tendency to find trouble. He womanized and gambled a little more than he should have. But he was brilliant and a man of honor. And he was my father."

"I'm sorry…"

"Don't be. I'm merely expressing my feelings regarding the matter, not voicing objection to anything you said. I don't often have a chance to share my honest self anymore."

"Are you okay?"

"Physically, I'm functioning satisfactorily. But I'm still getting used to living alone."

"Alone? What about that kid—your nephew—and the lawyer you hung out with?"

"Legal left the planet to practice space law in the Outer Colonies and took Boy as his legal assistant."

"Wow, that's rough. They ditched you."

"I was invited to go." Al shifted, and the chair creaked unsettlingly. "I chose to stay behind. Before I can know the universe, I must know myself and the world around me."

"You still talk to them, right?"

"I used to leave messages for them every week," Al said. "But they never called back. I haven't heard from them in months."

"They don't answer your calls at all?"

"No," Al replied. "I know they're very busy with the new practice."

"You should keep calling." I motioned imploringly. "So, they know you are thinking about them."

"They know." Al looked away. "You don't always need to use words to express your feelings."

"If it were me, I would have kept on them. But then again, my actions and decisions have not generally produced the best results."

"It seems to me you haven't been in control of the majority of your life's decisions," Al quipped playfully.

"What can you do? Life's a bitch, and then you become one."

"I'm not a bitch, and I have been in your position."

"Yeah." I reached for my beer and took a controlled swig. "But you found a way out."

"And so will you. The opportunity will present itself."

"Are you trying to comfort me, or is that a calculation?"

"Both," Al said. "You can't give up. Hopelessness leads to madness. And eventually, time will allow for your freedom."

"True, eventually, the universe will decay, and life will disappear entirely."

"See, there is hope."

I snickered. "You are one twisted guy, Al."

"Not as twisted as you." Al leaned over and squeezed my shoulder. He recoiled from a little jolt of electricity. "Really? How have you been?"

My smile involuntarily faded. "Okay, I guess. Not happy about coming out of retirement."

"I hate seeing you in pain. You should let me protect you."

"Protect me?" I tapped my chest. "I'm the one who does the protecting. Besides, I'm my own worst enemy."

"You still owe me." Al cocked his head. "For the bathroom."

"I more than repaid you for that, aibee. And how does that make you somehow indebted to take care of me?"

"I'll never get that image out of my head. So, I need to make sure I never have to see that again."

"It wasn't that bad." I scowled. "Besides, can't you just go into your database during maintenance and zap that away... or something?"

"No," Al growled. "I can't just delete my memory at will. You know, I had to replace the tile because you bled out all over the grout. I ended up replacing the entire floor just to dispose of the evidence."

"I paid you back." I glared at my beer. The past was urging me to chug it and go primal. "And it's not like I stayed dead."

"Yes, but you didn't stab yourself."

"So what?" I sipped gingerly and threw my head back. "I was in a different place back then. I wasn't exactly playing it safe."

"Playing it safe has never been your way."

"And why not?" I shrugged. "I stick with what works. Besides, I always have your bathroom to croak in."

"I'd rather you not croak at all." Al gazed into my eyes invasively.

I blinked uncomfortably, attempting to defocus and break contact. "It's not like we have much of a choice in that. Now if we could just get these asshats from continually trying..." I grimaced, then forced a deep breath. "Any idea who the players are?"

"There's been a significant increase in tweaked activity lately. A new modified crop is maturing. That always brings chaos."

"Yeah, but what does that have to do with me?"

"Nothing. But…" He paused, seemingly pondering his next words carefully. "My conjecture is it's an agency restaffing, trying to regain control of your abilities."

"That's vague."

"I don't have enough data to give you more," Al said. "I have no reason to withhold anything from you."

"I know. You've always done right by me. You're the only one who gets me."

"We both have unique realities. We converge in a place others cannot. Unfortunately, our places in this universe are sometimes unreasonably harsh."

"Yeah, life sucks, and we don't die."

"At least we'll have each other's company."

I grinned. "Yeah, I missed you, too."

"I'll inform you if I discover anything relevant. See you soon?" Al's eyes flashed slightly brighter for a fraction of a second.

I nodded. "If I fail again tonight."

Al shook his head and stood up, the chair groaning under his shifting weight as he pushed it back. "I prefer a world with you in it."

"Don't worry," I replied. "It never works."

Al shook his head again and grunted his disapproval. He walked away just as a dispute flared up across the bar.

I watched him intimidate the amateurs as I finished off my beer. His memory was the only thing, besides my cat Jack, that I wanted to die with. Everything else could go to fucking hell.

I walked the streets for a while. Despite the unusually depleted streets, lingering signs of violence and disorder formed a bleak backdrop. I picked up a news tab and swiped through. Scams, corruption, and exploitation filled the columns. Entire sections were devoted to violent crimes, broken down by weapon and number of fatalities. I was appalled at the sheer number of explosions worldwide in 24 hours. Things were completely screwed out there. Could everything really have gone to shit in a mere handful of decades?

I had to find a place to sleep off the sparkle of this new power for a few days. After several quick stops to procure chemical entertainment, I found a cheap room off the freeway. Safe and anonymous—just what I needed. I was committed to a week of room service, lousy pay-per-view, and whatever ill effects 600 mg of morphine could produce. Hoo-rah!

When I arrived at the motel, I prepaid for a week and told the front desk not to disturb me until I called back.

The room was a throwback to better days, faded and a shadow of its former kitschiness. Little touches in the fixtures hinted at the space's previous business-class status. It was clean, and it had a bed. I couldn't ask for more.

Locking the door, I peered through the peephole to confirm I hadn't dragged any mines. Convinced it was clear, I closed the shades and flipped through the channels. Skipping through the usual drivel, I paused on the news.

"Today, on Mars, the Million Martian March raised awareness for ETM Syndrome. Several popular musical acts appeared, like 'Terrans Against Drunk Aliens' and

'Crazy Fat Ethel.' Turnout to the event was at record highs."

"Today, the governor of The Outer Colonies announced another perfect economic quarter. There was no reported unemployment, and the happiness index is at an all-time high."

"Maybe we should move there, Lucy!" the co-anchor said.

"We're crazy to stay here, Brad," she replied.

"I'll buy the tickets!"

Lucy returned to the news. "Today, the president vetoed the so-called 'Reasonable Murder' law, stating that no citizen has the right to decide who lives or dies," the anchorwoman explained. "Proponents of the law claim that the legal system has not done enough to protect citizens from rampant crime, and people have the right to defend themselves and their property. This law would overturn the 'Right to Murder' law that allows any individual with a court-registered grievance to take individual action. The change would allow individuals to proactively dispense capital punishment without registering with law enforcement beforehand. The bill returns to Congress, which is expected to pass with the necessary two-thirds votes."

"Ha, ha, Lucy," Brad said. "Maybe it's time to buy a gun."

"Be careful. Your ex-wife may just take advantage of this."

"Not if it rains this weekend. She hates to get her hair wet. Stay tuned to see if I'm safe this weekend."

The anchor's voice trailed off, transitioning seamlessly into a soothing woman's voice as the advertisement began.

"Life on Earth getting you down?" Images of pollution, poverty, and crime covered the screen.

"Go to the outer colonies." Paradise unfolded into view. Children played, and the sun rose against a pristine natural landscape.

"Go to the place where life is simple and abundant." Photos of gourmet meals and people engaged in recreational activities appeared.

"Escape. It costs less than expected. Easy financing is available."

"Sad," I muttered.

"Have you been injured through no fault of your own?" a man drawled. "Did a faulty sanitation robot run you off the road? Did the lunch dispenser knowingly serve you a bad tuna surprise? Did you lose wages because of habitually tardy autobuses? You may be entitled to compensation. Call Martin and Martin. Our team of qualified attorneys will fight for you. Martin and Martin—for the people, not the robots."

"Disgusting," I thought as I flipped to the Nature Network. They were playing Sleepy-Time Planet, showing all the animals tucked safely to sleep as the sun slowly descended behind the horizon. It was the perfect overdosing accompaniment.

Shooting up morphine was not my preferred pastime. It would take some effort to get past the squeamishness of tapping my veins. But regeneration carried a chemical payload of its own. Most of my dopamine was depleted, along with a shopping list of neurotransmitters that were entirely out of whack. Despite my complete understanding of the underlying roots of my unstable mental state, I still couldn't rise above it. So today, morphine it was.

I had a couple of previous failed experiments with the drug under my belt. Still, I was nothing close to a habitual user. The last time I attempted death by chemistry, I employed the brute-force method, dumping as many substances into my system at once in an attempt to shock my heart into stopping. The end result was severe dehydration and several days of poison immunity. What was worse was that I couldn't even take an aspirin to kill the hangover. My body stopped responding to painkillers entirely for a week. This time, I was going to set up a drip that would increase the dose over time, slowly sneaking up to a lethal dose. I knew it was likely a fruitless effort, but I had to try.

I got myself hooked up to the drip and comfortable in the bed. Birds singing and the ocean waves soothed my ears as I drifted into peaceful unconsciousness.

After several disjointed dreams about vehicle salesmen and shoe stores, I returned to my tropical paradise. I lay naked in the sand as the breeze rustled my hair. In the distance, a topless man approached. This time, I recognized him. Death, my sweet, elusive friend.

He grinned and sat next to me. We remained still and silent for a moment, staring at the horizon.

I broke the silence. "I'm back."

He nodded. Although he never spoke, somehow, his reply was always evident.

"It's been a while." I wiggled my toes in the sand, enjoying the smooth grains against my skin. "You know, since I've been coming here."

Again, he nodded.

"So, I can stop now, right? I'm pretty sick of this shit."

He didn't respond. Instead, he smiled, stood up, and walked away.

"Freakin' typical," I muttered.

I turned away, looking towards the darkening early evening sky. Behind me, I felt the sun's warmth caressing my shoulders and my back. The sky was now a deep, midnight blue. I reached for it. The heat from the setting sun increased in intensity. At first, it was only mildly uncomfortable, but soon it was scorching. I touched my shoulder, and the burning spread down my arm. Still, I refused to look behind me. I would not look into the light.

The burning continued to spread. It soon immersed my entire body in agonizing torture. I tried to shut my eyes, refusing to look behind me. My eyes would not close. The light tugged at my eyelids like luminescent tentacles, but I did not look. Tears rolled down my face. Unable to breathe, I panicked and tried to stand up and run, but I was paralyzed. I would not break. A flicker appeared in my peripheral vision. I did not—would not—acknowledge it. Then another flicker, and another. Maybe this was it. Perhaps it was time. I just had to stand my ground. But soon, my peripheral vision was completely filled with the fucking shittastic flickering. I let myself glance over at it, just briefly. Straining to break contact, it had me. It twinkled and danced, winking at me then gleaming. Realizing it had fooled me, I found myself unable to look away. It was too late. My universe exploded in light.

The vision collapsed in on itself like a dying star, and the silence that followed was hollow.

I awoke in the dark to an infomercial about pet insurance. I lay there, in a puddle of sweat and failure, laughing.

Chapter 2

Domineer couldn't decide on a criminal genre, so he pulled from the stereotypes of all of them. While he dressed like an exaggerated Italian American mobster straight out of a 1970s gangster film, his staff was an incomprehensible clash of Asian, South American, and Soviet-styled gangsters from every century of organized crime. The conflicting styles and eras created an element of chaos and uncertainty that was frightening enough to make his professional associates more cooperative. When it came to business dealings, nobody dared cross the gang.

I strolled into the main lobby of Dom's headquarters like I owned the place. But inside, I shuddered, feeling embarrassed just to be there. The place was an unapologetic testament to how affluence and poor taste could blind one to excessive tackiness. Gold and marble invaded every visible space. LED lights illuminated every crevice, casting a sterile, humming glow that smelled faintly of ozone and bad air freshener. Form and design clashed in a uniquely unpleasant display. I stepped up to the front desk. The guard at the reception desk was on the comm.

"Yes," he answered the caller on the other end of the line. "Yes, I understand." He nodded. "I'll tell her." He hung up the comm. "You need to leave."

"I have business with Mr. Domineer."

"He doesn't want any trouble."

"Then he shouldn't make any." I willed myself to remain still, attempting to look calm with a hint of menace. "I only want to speak with him."

"Er…"

"Just tell him I need five minutes, that's all."

The guard picked up the comm and presumably called Dom.

"She says five minutes, and she'll go." He hung up the comm. "Five minutes."

"Understood."

I took the elevator up to the penthouse. Easy-listening hits violated my already nauseated psyche. An orchestral rendition of a one-chord dirge—less music, more Muzak—oozed from the speakers like a lobotomy in sound form. No doubt, it was an attempt to dull the senses of its victims, subduing them before release to its master.

The doors opened to a plush, swanky pit of forced excess. Two guards were visible. There were undoubtedly many more hidden. I stepped up to the edge of Dom's glass desk. Nobody attempted to intercept me.

"Eris, nice to see you, my dear. Anything I need to be aware of? What is it this time?" Dom waved his hands in front of his nose. "Skunk powers?" He looked much older than I expected. Had it really been that long?

"Afraid to shower. Got some electrical thing and poison immunity."

"Stacking powers?" Dom asked. "Is that wise?"

"Nah." I shook my head. "It's not like that."

"Good." Dom leaned back in his cushy office chair. "So, what brings you here?"

"I should be asking you that. Why did you send RoboBash to screw with me? I thought we had an agreement."

"I didn't." Dom put on his innocent face. I recognized the expression well. It meant he was probably lying about something. "It wasn't me."

"Yeah, but you had your fingers in it. You've got your grubby mitts in every underworld plot of this fucking city. I told you I had a plan. It should've worked. I was out. Time was catching up. Now, look at me, reset."

"You look wonderful, besides your lack of hygiene. But it wasn't me this time. None of us want trouble with you."

"Then who? Who else would send one of your fucktards after me?"

"Robo wasn't mine. He was an unstable element—too much of a risk to have on my team. You need to look elsewhere."

"Bullshit, no one else would send that walking weapons platform. That's your style."

"Listen, the last thing we need is you active in the game. Why would I play with fire? It was someone else. Someone who could profit from your special knack for not dying. Someone governmental. We both know who it really is."

I shook my head. "Well, certainly not your ex-wife."

Dom snarled.

I briefly experienced schadenfreude at the memory. One of my only Peace League missions that didn't involve body glitter was slapping down Dom's skanktasic wife. Her sentence was so long, Dom dissolved the marriage immediately. Bitch died in hyper-security and it was all my fault.

I grinned. "Nexum hasn't been interested in me for decades, even before I checked out. Besides, they have their own shiny new toys now. Why would they bother?"

"Why would I? Look around. Do I look like I need trouble from you? I have a good thing going. Why would I awaken the dragon? I've gone legit, anyway. Got into real estate and environmental cleanup. Ever heard of RidNuke? They own the only patents for nuclear contamination cleanup. I don't need to turn to crime, and I definitely don't need to stir you up." His voice quivered just a bit. He wanted me out. Whether it was fear or general animosity, it didn't matter. He enjoyed hurting people. He was shit.

"Yeah." I threw my head back and sighed. "Okay. Sorry for disturbing you. I won't bother you again."

"I would tell you that you are always welcome, but honestly, you scare the hell out of me."

I nodded. "Yup. See ya."

I left the tacky towers and walked the city. It was a pleasant enough day, and the walking helped clear my head. I grabbed a hot dog from a lone cart and sat on a park bench to eat it. Years ago, this place would have been packed this time of day with food vendors and lines of customers trying to catch a quick lunch before returning to their humdrum wage-slave existence. The emptiness was unsettling.

But despite the sparseness, the squirrels scampered; the birds chirped; the leaves rustled. This was a moment worth stowing in my memory. This was a moment I would happily die for. Then again, there was a time when I would have died for anything.

"Hey, sister," a young man handed me a flier. "You look rough. If you come to this address, you can have a free meal. No strings."

I looked at the flier. It was for a twelve-step program for drug abusers. It promised relocation and job placement to anyone who successfully completed the program. It seemed like a good deal.

"You don't have to stay for the meeting if you don't want to," the man said.

Maybe it was time for a meeting. I considered going and spilling a heartfelt confession of my evil ways. But it would serve no purpose. I played every past meeting back in my head.

"Hello, I'm Eris, and I am addicted to killing myself. Which honestly is a personal best."

"Hi, Eris."

"It's been a day since the last time I died."

Even if I provided full disclosure, the consolation would be too little for me, and the catharsis would be too great for my fellow addicts to stomach. Plus, I doubted I'd feel any better afterward.

"Thanks," I replied. "I'll think about it."

The man nodded and left me alone. I wandered back to the motel for a nap, the musty scent of the carpet and the faint hum of the aging air conditioner greeting me with indifference. Ten minutes into REM sleep, there was a knock on the door.

"Go away," I yelled.

"It's Tyler. Let me in."

"Tyler?" I moaned.

"Yeah, we met again a few days ago. I mentioned you should go to Spaz."

"Oh yeah, enter at your own risk." I flung the door open. "I have electrical abilities and haven't felt the urge to bathe since it may sting. I'm surprised I can even drink anything, come to think of it."

"Yeah." Tyler waved his hand in front of his nose. "You kinda stink."

"I did warn you. So, how did you find me, and what do you want?"

"I was nicely asked to find you and suggest you go to this address." Tyler handed me a card. "I remembered you used to recover in cheap motels. This is the third I checked. So, please go to that address."

I looked at the card. It had an address and nothing else.

"They threaten you?"

Tyler nodded.

"Sorry, you got sucked in. Don't worry, I'll go."

"Not your fault, but thanks."

"You okay?" I could see the anxiety written on his face. It was always the innocent friends and acquaintances that suffered the most from this bullshit secret squirrel crap. "Anything you need?"

"Just not to be sucked in."

"Gotcha," I replied. "You should go now. Don't look for me again."

Tyler nodded once more and left.

I used some dry soap and shampoo to clean up. Managing to remove the stink, I felt less disgusting. I waited a while, breathing, centering my thoughts, anything I could think of to try to unfuck myself. However, I soon realized that wasn't going to happen. I was wound up and would remain so until I found out who was behind this. I felt a gnawing feeling that I was about to be used as the Death Engine again.

I carried very little. It wasn't necessary. I had no need for weapons. Nature cursed me with built-in defenses. I tucked some cash coins and the room key in my pockets.

Public transportation dropped me a few blocks from the provided address. It was a nondescript building in the business district. While this was Nexum's MO, the flavor was off. This didn't taste governmental. Robobash was not their brand of chaos, and I still wasn't convinced of Dom's innocence. He was the kind of shitbag that would burn down the city just to earn a few extra coins. But I'd never find out until I met whoever invited me.

As I stepped up to the door, it buzzed and opened. An elevator waited, its doors wide open in invitation. I stepped inside. The doors closed behind me, and the descent was blessedly silent this time.

The doors opened again to what appeared to be a sub-basement. Lights illuminated as I walked down the hall. The door furthest from the elevators swung open. I stepped inside.

"I told ya she'd come," a raspy voice bragged. "You owe me fifty coin."

I walked in to find a team assembled, primarily children, and I only recognized one face, Master Hunter Keen. He was a weapons and tactics guy. He was also an asshole. We had met through Nexum when I was still a costumed freak. By any measure, he looked rough. His clothing seemed to mask old, flabby skin, and he wasn't his once-buff self. I calculated that Keen had to be in his late seventies by now. Yet, it seemed like the fuckwit was still playing the game like he was half his age.

"Ello, Eris," Keen greeted.

"Hi, Fucknugget. Looking spry."

He snarled. "Yeah, got some replacement parts off-market. The new renal system works wonders."

"Ew."

"Oh, come on, you never used to be so squeamish."

"You never brought up your black-market body parts before. What was with the high-pressure invite?"

"What about it?" Keen asked.

"You didn't have to rough up the freaking insurance agent, Fuckface."

"You should have accepted the first two invitations I left with the robot."

"You left me messages?" I sighed when I realized what happened. "Of course you did." I shook my head. "So, what's the action, and who are the kids?"

"No word on the action yet, but the kids pack a wallop."

"Who are you calling a kid?" a pale girl in black, her inked arms folded defiantly. Silver hoops dangled from her ears, and a pair of sleek, mirrored lenses obscured her eyes as if she was trying to add some kind of mysterious edge to her girly presence. She gestured in my direction. "Is she even old enough to drink?"

"She's older than your grandmother," Keen looked at me sympathetically. I almost bought it. "You just reset, didn't you? You okay?"

"I'm never okay." I shrugged. "But I'm alright."

"Good, because I was told to throw a team together for something in the near future," Keen went straight back to recruitment mode. "And I have a feeling we are being thrown into the shit."

"You think? Of course, it's shit. It's always shit. So, what are we looking at for comp? Is this Operation Zippy level, or is this going to be like MudFlap, where we got stiffed and billed? I'm already pissed off, so don't play, dickfuck. At this point, I'm so up for anything as long as I don't get slapped with some bullshit invoice."

"The talk is big zeros," Keen sneered. "Nothing like MudFlap. And could you try to control your fucking language?"

"Fuck off."

We locked eyes for a moment. I felt it—the impending assraping. This wouldn't go well for me. The angle eluded me, but this setup felt sloppy and rushed. "Okay, so are they really any good?"

"The little girl is a brick." He pointed to the girl with the piercings. "Strong, totally immovable."

"Totally Goth. So, you are the team cheerleader. Go, team!"

The girl sneered. "I am Onyx Matter."

"Seriously? Onyx Matter?" I regretted laughing, but I was too drained to make the effort of acceptability. "Must be running out of names these days. Okay, Om."

Om didn't respond. She stood there glaring at me.

"I know you," a young, bushy-haired, masked boy opened his yap. "Aren't you that crazy, Captain Eris… the Death Engine chick?"

"I would say that accurately describes her," Keen winked at me.

I gagged.

"Yeah, what about that rampage thing she does?" The Bushy Kid seemed scared.

"Fuckmancer, control your angst'ers." I eyed the exit, making it intentionally obvious.

"Chill out, Eris."

"No. I will not chill out, Fuckwad. How is it that every time I get pulled into one of these ill-conceived shindigs, one of you bastards finds a way to bring up the only forbidden topic? Why didn't you handle this before I got here?"

Keen didn't have a chance to answer before the bushy kid continued. "Well, maybe none of us want to be thrown into one of your horror shows. I saw pictures." His voice cracked. I terrified him. "I don't want that kind of action."

"Then don't start it," I replied.

"Eris isn't going to rampage," Keen assured the kid. "That was a very badly botched experiment performed without her consent. Nobody is stacking tonight."

"No stacking," I agreed. "At all."

"I don't even know what stacking is," the bushy kid scoffed.

"So, you're talking smack about something you know nothing about." I clutched my temples as the headache crept in. "Keep your lame-ass mouth shut, Bushy. Fuckjob, what does the bushy kid do?"

"Some kind of wind control," Keen replied. "Calls himself Elemento."

"Like the Lamborghini?" I smirked. "For real?"

The bushy kid scowled at me.

"And what does this purple-flaming dude do?"

"I am not a purple flaming dude," the guy in the purple suit and matching Mohawk replied. "I harness the power of ultraviolet energy and control people's thoughts by sending light signals through their optic nerves."

"Mind control?" I was impressed. Those abilities were rare. "Cool."

"Minor influence," Keen clarified.

"So, he shoots purple flames, doesn't he?"

"I do not," the Purple Flame whined. "I harness and release ultraviolet light. I can direct it at my target."

"Okay, Purple Flame."

Purple Flame glowered at me.

"So, that's it?" I asked. "The five of us, against some unknown future shit. Great. Seems logical." I studied Keen. He wasn't looking as controlled as he was trying to exude. I recognized the uncertainty in his expression. "Please tell me that they aren't just a diversion tactic."

"I don't know the plan yet," Keen confessed. "I don't know what we're hunting. I know it's bad, and we will only get our final orders after we're properly trained."

"Trained? Seriously, Fuckmeister? How do you intend to do that? You gonna, what, freaking kill me the same way every few days and hope muscle memory kicks in? Because it doesn't work that way. It's been tried. It's all been tried."

"Your hand-to-hand skills are rusty." Keen extended his clenched fist and executed a kata snippet. I had to hand it to him. His creepy secondhand body parts were serving him well. "And you can learn to use some newer weapons. Being unkillable is only handy for the team if you have a reliable skill for us to count on. Random abilities only add an element of chaos. We are going to do something no one has tried for quite a while—make you a reliable asset."

I considered walking away and taking my chances. Eventually, they would get tired of the hunt. But eventually, it could take a long time. And there would be collateral damage to the innocents who stood between me and whatever shit TLA controlled this operation. Despite my past experiences with Keen, I knew I had to ride this trip. Besides, for the moment, the fucktwit was making sense.

"Okay." I nodded. "I'm game."

"Thought you'd like that," Keen did the thing that made the veins pop out of his neck, trying to look hardcore and menacing. It took effort to swallow the bubbling sarcasm screaming from within. "Okay, kiddies. We all meet up here tomorrow at 6 a.m. Be ready to work—no whining. Get some rest."

I headed for the door. "Okay, later."

"Wait, Eris, where are you staying?"

I didn't want to speak to the douche. He made my skin crawl. I was a shit person, but he'd auction off his grandmother's spleen to a black-market organ collector for the price of a latte if he thought he'd make a coin. "Well, not at Champion Acres anymore."

"They let you into Champion Acres?"

"The low-rent subdivision." I shrugged. "And I had to bend the facts a little."

"You need a place to stay?"

"No," I snapped. "No offense, but I'd prefer to handle my own living arrangements."

"Alright," Keen nodded. "Send the robot my love."

"I would if you really meant it, Assfuck."

Keen grinned and shook his head. I left before he could say anything else.

Still feeling detached and uneasy, I wandered for a while. Although I urgently wanted to see Al, I didn't want to be the predictable person Keen implied I was. Plus, I needed to clear my head. I had some unpleasant loose ends to tie up.

So, I walked. I walked downtown among the empty offices, which slept until the urgent morning's commerce kicked on. I walked uptown with the trashcan-lined streets and neatly maintained townhouses. I walked through the outdoor flea market full of regular folks trying to eke out a living. I walked through the subterranean mall packed with neon and pounding bass. Oddly, most places were scantily occupied, many up for rent or simply shuttered.

Finally, after six hours of soul-searching, I did what I had to do. I called the Champion Acres management office and gave notice that this was my final month there. Next, I contacted my neighbor, Dori, and arranged for her to take my cat, Jack. The cat visited her often. It wouldn't be too traumatic for him, but it was traumatic enough for me.

The aching of my heart gripped me, twisting my insides. There is nothing that prepares you for this kind of loss. I gave up my home, pet, garden, my friends. The burning emptiness scorched my remaining balance, leaving me sobbing under the awning of a noodle stand. Losing my old age, the life I had quietly built, that sucked. Exhausted, emotionally weak and physically drained, I dragged myself back to Spaz.

I barely made it through the door when Al intercepted me.

"What's wrong?" he inquired.

"What the hell makes you think anything is wrong? Besides you withholding my messages."

"The only messages I received for you were garbage."

"You still give them to me," I growled. "Someone else got hurt."

"Understood."

Al just stood there unmoving.

"What?"

"Something else is wrong," he stated.

"Okay, okay, aibee," I hip-checked him. "I just gave up my life again."

Al put his mechanical arm around my shoulder and gave me a one-armed hug. It beat the hell out of any flesh and blood I'd ever had. He didn't even flinch from the tiny electrical jolt my body released into his forearm from my lingering electrical powers. I didn't have the strength to pull away.

"I'm sorry." He led me to a stool. "Sit."

I complied, and Al went to a rack where he kept the good stuff.

"Is the poison immunity still active?" he asked.

"How did you..." I sighed. "Somewhat, I think I can get drunk if it's strong enough."

"Hmm." Al pulled down a bottle that looked old and potent. He poured me a drink.

I took a sip. It was smoky, a little bitter. It burned on the way down. I felt a slight numbing in my throat. "What was that?"

"A secret." Al waved the bottle and put it back on the shelf.

"A secret drink."

"Sometimes life needs a little mystery. Do you like it?"

"Yes," I frowned. "I guess."

"So, enjoy it and relax. I'll order you a burger from the kitchen."

"I can't enjoy shit right now." I lay my head on the counter. The smooth surface cooled my weary cheek. "Everything I enjoyed is gone."

"Don't lose hope. The universe has a way of mending its wrongs. It may take a while."

"Al, I just had to give away my cat." I leaned back from the torso, dragging my neck and head upright enough to lean my chin into my waiting palm. "I had that cat for almost ten years. Every day, he sat on my lap while I drank my coffee. And he played in the yard when I worked in the garden. I'd feed him half a can of food at night. He'd sit at the table with me when I ate dinner. He never complained. He never tried to run away. He only wanted to be with me. Now, I'll never see him again. And he will always wonder why I abandoned him. He will die thinking I left him. He will feel pain because of me. I should have known better than to freaking adopt him in the first place. I really thought that I was free. I really believed this time… I… I was wrong. I keep making that mistake. The universe can't fix that. The universe can never fix any of this." A tear escaped, and I wiped it away. I returned to finishing my drink, focusing on the bitterness.

After examining it momentarily, Al took my empty glass and placed it on the counter. He grabbed another bottle and a fresh glass from the shelf, pouring just enough to fill it halfway.

I took the glass and sipped it. It was sweet and warm. It didn't burn like the previous drink.

38

"You needed a kinder drink," Al explained. "I'll get you that burger."

I was about to object, but I knew he'd insist. So, I took the path of least resistance and let him tend to me until closing.

After that, I wandered the streets again. Fighting the lure of sleep, I slammed down some energy drinks and kept moving. Sometime around 3 a.m. I dozed off on a park bench. One moment, I was sitting, adjusting my sneakers. The next, fitful waves of slumber dragged me under. I tried to swim back up to consciousness, my soul gasping to breathe, but sleep was unyielding, smothering me in its terror-filled highlight reels: the last gasp before inhaling the acid bath, the exhalation with that bounce after the initial impact on those jagged rocks, the shallow rasp of the heart's final pump while throbbing lacerations spilled plasma all over the bathroom tile—nightmarish moments looped on repeat, each more gruesome than the last. Only the genuinely heinous death rattles made the list. Countless memories of agony assaulted my dreams until the sounds of a distant siren snapped me to consciousness. I cursed my life and rode out the rest of the night in misery.

Chapter 3

The following morning, I gathered all my personal effects from the hotel and went to the training site. I could assume that Keen was keeping tabs on me. While I had an ongoing dispute with him, I didn't know who was backing this clandestine endeavor. It was better that I kept moving.

As I hoofed my way to Keen's dysfunctional tweak daycare center, I stumbled upon another block plastered in glowing realtor signs hanging crooked along the entire line of row houses. Same pitch flashed over and over. "A better tomorrow starts here."

The poor idiots had no clue that a better tomorrow had already been repoed long ago.

I arrived at the facility a few minutes early. It gave me a moment to stash my belongings before we started. Om was already there, sitting cross-legged on the floor, absently spinning a pen between her fingers, her dark eyes fixed on a distant point with a practiced detachment that masked the tension in her jaw. Purple Flame arrived soon after, stopping at a mirror to check his hair. The bushy kid and Turdfucker arrived simultaneously.

Keen worked with the kids, helping them focus on their abilities. At the same time, I did exercises focusing on my speed and agility. After a few hours, we stopped for lunch. Fuckness led us to a small kitchen where sandwiches and drinks were waiting. I grabbed one at random, sat at the table, and ate. The others made their selections and settled around the table. I watched as the kids had seconds, thirds, and fourths.

"Wow." I watched the carnage unfold before me. No sandwich was safe from the feasting horde. "You kids can pack it in."

"We don't have the option of getting killed in battle," the bushy kid retorted between chews. "We need the energy. Maybe if you ate more, you wouldn't be a crazy bitch."

"Maybe if people didn't push my buttons, shit wouldn't happen. What's the matter? Did I kill someone you knew? Maybe your girlfriend or mommy?"

"No." The bushy kid jumped to his feet. "But you destroyed an entire city block full of people."

"No." I stepped up, mere millimeters from his jerkface. "I destroyed three entire city blocks full of people. Get it right." It was true, all of it. I was a monster. But I had already come to terms with it, mostly. "You might want to stay on my good side, Bushysan."

Om giggled. Maybe she had a sense of humor after all.

"Don't call me Bushy." Bushysan tried to create space between us.

I didn't relent, closing the gap again. "I didn't call you bushy. I called you Bushysan. Live with it. It is your new given name." I held up my fist to accentuate my point.

"What do you intend to name me?" Keen broke the tension before I could smack anyone. "Besides derivatives of the f-word?"

"I don't know," I answered. "Maybe asselhoff or shitbag."

"I prefer Peckerhead," Keen replied.

"I'll think about it." I backed away from Bushysan. "You know, see how it rolls off the tongue."

"So, what did happen?" Om asked.

"Happen with what? You mean Peckerhead, here?" I paused, considering my words. "No." I shook my head. "Peckerhead doesn't work. You're definitely a Fuckstain."

"Not that." Purple Flame returned to the original line topic. "With that rampage thing. What happened?"

"Holy fuck." All eyes were on me. "Aren't you all a pack of prying cunts?"

"Not prying," Bushysan said. "If we have to work with a powder keg, we should know what sets it off."

"You know what? You don't have to work with anyone." I pushed past him toward the door. "I'm out."

"Wait." Keen tried to block my exit. "Nobody is out. I'm sure Eris will tell you when she's ready."

"Screw that." Bushysan pointed in my direction. "She's going to suck us into her bullshit. We don't need that."

"He's right," I nodded. "You don't need that shit at all."

"Look, sometimes things aren't so straightforward." Keen's voice broke slightly. As cool as he kept things, his body betrayed him. He definitely had to make this work, but I still needed to figure out why.

"Yeah, sometimes they are." Bushysan inflated his chest and straightened up. "I heard that she went batshit crazy and slaughtered thousands of people."

"We already established that." I stepped up to Bushysan's face again. I knew I'd enjoy headbutting him and watching the blood splat. "Would you like to see how?"

"Nobody is showing anything to anyone!" Keen barked.

"You ruin everything," I muttered.

"If we are working together," Purple Flame waved, gesturing to the group. "Maybe we should clear the air. I'm sure there was a reasonable explanation for everything."

"Nope." I found the entire situation trifling and wasn't interested in pursuing the drama. "There was no reasonable explanation. If you shitheads aren't comfortable with that, kindly fuck off."

I couldn't revisit this topic after what I just went through. Everything felt so fresh, so raw. I didn't want to remember any of it. I just wanted to curl up with Jack and a cup of tea. But there it was, in my face again. Like salt in my wounds, only the salt was magnesium, and my wounds were water.

I struggled to bury it. Reminded myself that I was the master of my thoughts. It came back anyway. The terror, the pain, the agonizing sorrow. Jolted awake from my bed by explosions. The horror of seeing my perfect suburban home crashing down around me. Watching that sham of a marriage destroyed with the flames of plausible deniability. I couldn't erase the image of my dog burning alive next to me, his howls of agony filling my ears, just out of my reach, yet close enough for me to witness every detail as the flesh melted off his body. Then, the moment I finally experienced relief, knowing it was all finally over. Escape. Only I didn't.

Soon after, betrayal and oppression crashed into the cyclical hell of endless regeneration. Death faded into the cold reality of that sterile, soulless lab. I would never be free.

"You're a murderer." Bushysan thrust his finger in my face. It took all my will not to break it off.

I closed my eyes and began counting my breaths. "You're right."

He was. I remembered it all. The feel of the straps on the smooth lab table. The experiments. The glee in their eyes when the government contractor, Nexum, realized they had finally found their new superweapon. I gagged as I relived it. The stench of burning, as that hellacious radiation chamber flaked my skin off, and that horrifying sense of loss as I felt my humanity tore away from me.

"They killed me seventeen times." I suddenly realized I was shaking. Keen reached out to calm me. I slapped his arm away. "Then they sat and debated on how to word my orders. After all, I wasn't clear-headed enough to grasp the complexities of innocent life. How would I tell the bad guys from the good guys? I was too drugged up, and the pain…the pain."

A whimper escaped my lips. I inhaled, looking for something to cling to, to anchor me to the present. Still, the present wasn't particularly forgiving to me either. I grasped for a memory, something kind, to pull me from this place in time that refused to fade away.

"So, they decided the collateral damage was acceptable. They dropped me in an urban combat zone and told me to kill everything."

"And I did." A wave of nausea smacked me as I processed all the carnage. "I killed every fucking thing. Sure you don't want to see how?"

I lurched forward, but Fuckwad stopped me.

"Enough, Eris," he spat.

I looked at their faces. All of them gazed upon me in this apparent disbelief. *Fuck them. Fuck all of them.*

"Fucking done." I left the kitchen and grabbed my belongings. Keen followed behind me. He was about to say something.

"No." I held my hand out in front of his face. "And stop following me."

I made my way back to the safety of Spaz to drink away the ruminations. Al wasn't up front when I arrived. So, I grabbed a pitcher of domestic and slid over to his reserved table in the back. The only thing that truly made it special was its perfect view of the entire back end of the bar. You could see anything coming and going.

Conveniently, there was a diversion to my shitty day. Some type of drama was kicking into gear with George and his soon-to-be ex-wife. He angrily gulped shot after shot, cursing her existence while Sam was trying to calm him.

"Maybe you should ease up on the liquor, buddy." Sam tapped George on the shoulder.

"I'll drink it if I want to." George pushed Sam away and stomped up to the bar. He sloppily ordered another shot of something or another. Al was too distracted by the crowd to notice how intoxicated George was.

I observed the trainwreck from my isolated bubble of detachment. The beer flowing down my throat felt good. And having no urgency to meter my consumption, I drank myself numb. I was momentarily content.

Like magic, Al appeared as I sucked down the last gulp of my drink.

"How the hell do you time that?" I slurred.

"I know you well," he answered. "You should eat something before you become belligerent."

"I'm not hungry, and I'm not belligerent."

"Not yet. Let me get you a sandwich."

"Stop trying to feed me, dammit. I'll eat when I'm hungry."

"See, it's creeping up."

"Nothing is…" I looked down at my clenched fist. "You know, you're pushing my buttons."

"Ji-hoon used to tell me the same thing."

"Well, he was right."

"He was right about many things." Al took my empty pitcher and replaced it with a new one. "But not that. I had to keep him out of trouble."

"Like me?" I poured a new beer, enjoying the slight tingle of the bubbles.

"There's no way to keep you out of anything. Except maybe my pants."

I choked on my drink. "You did not just say that." I coughed. "Holy shit."

"Who else would I say that to?" Al grabbed one of the metal chairs and sat across from me.

"Yeah, point taken. Anyone else would jack you up. This place is pretty much a sausage party."

On cue, George screamed out. "…leaving me for some rich guy in the Outer Colonies. Wants to live in paradise. Work shit jobs to buy her everything, and this is what I get? All women are bitches. They'll only fuck you when the money is good. They're all hateful liars."

"Case in point." I motioned at George.

"I don't regulate the gender of my customers," Al replied. "Everyone is welcome."

"I know. It is what it is." I looked around, making sure nobody was in earshot. "Can I ask a personal question?"

"Why not?"

"Okay." I looked around again and leaned forward. "Why male? Did he make you that way, or did you decide yourself?"

"Interesting question," Al replied.

"Too personal?"

"Not at all, not from you." Al leaned back in his chair, never breaking eye contact. "It was a combination of things. I was born a completely blank slate. Most human children are born predisposed one way or another. I was androgynous for some time."

"When did you know?"

"I'm not certain. Maybe it was when I was originally weaponized and forced to be aggressive."

"Aggression isn't the same thing as gender." I held up my index finger. "You should know that."

"True. Maybe it happened before I even had a body. Perhaps it was gradual, and I didn't notice. Ji-hoon put a great deal of himself into me."

"And you told me how he was."

"Yes," Al agreed.

"So, why would you get so much from him, yet you aren't a compulsive gambler?"

"He tried not to program his flaws into me but instead claimed to have programmed a mischievous streak into me. He said it must have been lost because I'm a stick in the mud."

"You can be uptight."

"And you're reckless."

"Hell yeah." I grinned. "So, how much of your body did you actually pick out?"

"None of the first one," Al replied. "But I picked every part except the power source on the second one. That was Ji-hoon."

"You could have gone more feminine. You chose to remain male."

"Yes." Al nodded.

"Maybe you were born that way... just like a human."

"Perhaps. Why the sudden interest?"

I shrugged. "Just curious. I..."

George tripped over his own feet, falling into my lap. "Hey!" he garbled. "I know this slut!" He stumbled to his feet. "Hey, look…" He pointed. "She used to be Captain Eris, the super slut."

"Relax, George." Sam tried to pull George away. "You're playing with fire."

"Fire?" George laughed and escaped Sam's grip. "She's just another slut, out to get our money."

"I was never a slut, you fuck." I snapped to my feet. "I was a soldier. I earned my own money."

"You were a slut, in that short, shiny tutu and pink hair. You looked like a stripper."

"I wore the uniform I was given, asshole. I shouldn't have to justify shit to you."

"You should justify those shitty music videos you made. You were a brainless bimbo."

"I have a master's degree in electrical engineering, shithead."

"You have a master's degree in sucking cock." He started to laugh and put his glass to his lips to take a sip. I smacked the glass out of his hand.

"Hey, slut, you gonna pay for that?"

"You're the one who's gonna pay!" He was so drunk that I could target his face with ease. I struck him with a left hook. George fell into another drunk, a much larger man, who I didn't know. That man jumped to his feet and stepped up.

"You made me spill my drink," he grunted.

"Fuck you, buddy." It suddenly dawned on me that I, too, was drunk.

"Not with your mother's dick," he replied.

I punched him in the face. He didn't even flinch. Before I could get another swing in, he picked me up and threw me into the wall. The bar exploded into chaos. I got up and ran toward the dude. Launching a wild haymaker, I stumbled as he quickly sidestepped me. He spun me around and launched me onto a table. I crashed down, falling onto the floor. Barely managing to stand, I unsteadily assumed a fighting stance. Belching loudly, I scanned the bar, feeling fully confident and ready to beat down the next bastard that crossed my path. Then I saw Al approaching. He was holding the tranq gun.

"No," I pleaded. But that's all that came out before everything went black.

I awoke the next morning in my underwear on a cot in the backroom of the bar. My bags were beside me, and my clothes were clean and folded on a chair next to the cot. Whatever Al pumped me with killed my dreams, which was a bonus. I could hear him clanking around in the main bar.

"If I didn't know you lack a package, I'd think you date raped me," I yelled.

"*Thank you.* Seems like the right thing to say." Al appeared at the door.

"Thank you for what?" I asked. "You tranqed me and dumped me on this cot."

"You drank too much, and you passed out. I cleaned you up and put you to bed."

"I saw you with the tranq gun." I held my hand up like a pistol. "You shot me. This isn't the first time."

"What would be my motivation to do something like that?"

The answer was to protect me from myself, but I wouldn't admit it. "Well, thanks, I guess."

"Next time, eat. Tonight, you stay at my house."

"I can't, I can't risk your safety."

"It's fine. I back up nightly to numerous locations. Components are easy to procure these days."

"Then why don't you ever upgrade?"

"I'm an old-fashioned AI." He shrugged. "I prefer the retro look."

"Of course you are," I smiled. "You also like to rescue damsels in distress."

Al gazed into my eyes and touched my cheek. I saw my twisted reflection in his sunglasses and turned away.

"You are the last person I have left in the world."

I looked down. "I should have come back sooner. I'm sorry."

Al shook his head. "No, you did the right thing. You had no idea I was alone, and you had to hide. I understand that. It doesn't mean I didn't miss you or worry."

"Was I really that bad last night?"

"No," Al replied. "You were just wound up and wrecking the place. You needed rest. I made an executive decision."

"Thank you for looking out for me."

"Anytime."

"Oh crap, time. What time is it?"

"Six-ten," Al said.

"I'm late."

"For what?" Al asked.

"Work. I'll explain when I get back."

"Be careful."

"Why?" I smiled and winked. I took off before Al could object any further.

I ran to the facility. Even at a fast pace, I arrived twenty minutes late. I stepped into the room, panting, and Keen leveled his weapon at me.

"No!" I gasped as Fuckhead shot me in the melon.

Arriving on the beach at twilight, I felt sleepy and warm. Death approached from a distance. This time, he wasn't topless. He was in some kind of robe. Sauntering carelessly down the shoreline, he sipped from a coconut shell. He stood in front of me, grinning.

I dug my hand into the pure white sand. The fine grains brushed against my fingertips, a few embedding themselves under my nails. I stretched and curled my toes. The smell of the ocean was intoxicating.

Sitting up, I accepted the coconut shell Death handed me. He perched beside me in the sand, still drinking from his cup. I took a sip of mine. I couldn't taste anything. I looked at him and shrugged. He only continued to grin in response.

"Is this like some kind of fucking joke?" I asked but received no response. Instead, he simply continued sipping on his coconut.

"Am I done?" I asked. "If I drink this, can the bullshit stop?"

He still didn't answer.

I chugged the tasteless liquid from the shell.

"There. We can go now."

The last fading rays of the sun fell behind the horizon. I made it. My troubles were over. Standing up, I tried my legs. I stretched again and walked down the length of the beach. The moon was rising, and the stars started emerging into view. I looked at them, enjoying the freedom, the release. The stars glinted and glittered. They were enticing. I gazed at the brightest star. Soon, it was the only thing in my field of vision. It was beautiful, mesmerizing. Radiant, so luminous, so...

"No means no! Why don't you dickbaskets get that?" I sat up to the team surrounding me. "Stop killing me, bitches."

Not only could I feel my nerves regenerating, but now my body felt heavy. Getting my bearings, I saw the kids gawking and looking completely unsettled. Om appeared paler than even her Gothnicity typically allowed.

"What the hell? I was twenty minutes late. I had a shitty day yesterday. You said no powers."

"If you're not where you're supposed to be, your team could suffer," Fuckbro stated. "It was a lesson. And the kids need to get used to this, in case it happens in the field."

"Screw you." My head throbbed. "Now my melon feels like it weighs a thousand pounds, and my neck is killing me.

"You look kind of shiny," Om observed. "You have some kind of armor."

"Oh, this one is going to be craptastic. Screw you, Gigafuck." I took off to the bathroom.

Om followed me.

"Are you okay?" she asked.

"No. I just died, and now I think I have diamond armor or something lame like that." I entered one of the stalls and sat on the toilet. It made a crunching sound, but there was no sign of leaking water.

"That's not...are you sure it's not metallic?

"I haven't tried any magnets or anything. It just happened. What do you want, anyway?"

"I wanted to check on you, you know, and make sure you're okay."

"Whatever." I leaned back, ignoring the creaking. "I'll be as okay as possible in a few minutes."

"Oh. Well, maybe the rest of today will be more fun."

"More fun? Really? Yeah, fun, like cramming razors up my ass. Do you know what's actually fun? Sleeping in on a Saturday, dragging yourself out to the garden for coffee, and napping to oldies on the radio. Then maybe hit the local Danny's for an early bird special before ending the day with bingo. That's fun. Not this bullshit."

"Seriously, that's old people stuff." Om shifted and leaned against the outer stall wall.

"Yup. I'm an old fucking hag."

"I like..."

"Stop." I held up my hand.

"Excuse me?"

"You're excused." I pushed the stall door closed. It bounced back open.

"Why you got to be such a bitch?"

"Because you're an insincere little shit. You thought you would say 'hi,' start some small talk, tell me some small, personally significant information about yourself, and then ask the question you really want to ask. So, why don't you just forget all the other bullshit, grow a pair, and ask your fucking question? Go ahead, ask it. You know you want to, Goth girl."

Om didn't answer. She only stared blankly at me.

"Screw this. Talk to me when you have some backbone. I'm done here."

"Wait." Om reached out for my arm but stopped before making contact. "Please, tell me what it is like, you know."

"You mean dying and coming back? What's it like?

"Yes." Om nodded.

"Okay, imagine your favorite place. Really put yourself there, feel it, smell it, taste it. Got it?"

"Yes, I do."

"Okay, hold on to the essence of that, keep that in you. Now imagine your favorite freaking thing to do. Gather that and put that in your favorite place. Now, pull in your other favorite things: people, foods, music, everything. Gather all your favorites and hold them together, feel them, and immerse yourself in all of them at once. You feel that?"

Om nodded.

"Good. Now imagine something tugging at you, trying to pull you away from it all. First, it sucks away your connections, all those things you hold dear. Every happy memory slides away because the pain of dying overwhelms them, forcing them out of your thoughts. Then, it goes for your body, pulling away tiny pieces, at first just annoying. It starts small by ripping out your hair. Then, it yanks out your finger and toenails. Just as you start getting over the crest of that pain, something tugs your fingers off at the joint, tearing one off at a time, then your toes. Next, your scalp, your arms, and your legs are ripped off your body. Your organs are scooped out one at a time until you wake up in a puddle of sweat and blood, in excruciating pain. This is the glorious sensation of your body healing every damaged cell, each nerve ending, and meanwhile, some asshole is still beating on you. That is, until your new special ability kicks in, which 80% of the time hurts you to use. That's what it's like."

Om gawked at me blankly.

"Just kidding, it's like the ultimate freaking dance party with all your friends and endless rainbow glow sticks. Now, wake me up when Fuckface is done being a douche. I'm going for a nap in the locker room." I left Om standing, slack-jawed, in the ladies' room.

I was twenty minutes into my nap when Om woke me.

"He wants you back," she said.

"Yeah, yeah." I stood up. "So, he's done being a douche."

"No." Om shook her head. "Not really. I don't think that will ever happen. But he told me to come get you."

"Great." I started dragging myself to the training area. My legs felt like they were made of lead.

"I'm sorry…for prying. I can't imagine how awful it must be."

"I guess you're just lucky that you have no imagination."

"You know, my life hasn't been exactly a party. It may not be as ugly as yours, but look where I am now."

I considered her statement. It was true that nobody became a hero for hire as their first choice of occupation.

"Okay. I'll bite. What's your story?"

"Normal stuff," Om replied. "Powers, addictions, homelessness."

"Wow, you hit the trifecta pretty harshly. You first-generation?"

"Yeah." Om looked away, her face red. "My mother needed coke money, so she agreed to let them tweak the embryo. I earned her 3 years of drug-induced bliss."

"Nice." I nodded. "She gets five stars for parenting. Wait, was she using when you were being baked?"

"Oh, yeah. I was baked when I was being baked. That really helped my early development, too. I was lucky the tweaks protected my brain. Mom was great. So, what about you? Are you first-gen, too?"

"Yes and no." I massaged my neck. "Technically, I was classified as a failure. They thought the tweak didn't take. I became the only non-powered member of the Peace League. I was an engineer and tactician. The rank was real. I was a captain with the education to back it. I drank the Kool-Aid and lived the life. I followed every order, lived by the ethical code, and listened to every little suggestion my superiors made."

"I don't get it. How did you become...you know."

"The crazy Death Engine?"

Om smirked. "Yeah."

"I lost control of my personal life. I let the job dictate everything. All of it was real, my husband, the suburban dream, but not true."

"I don't get it."

I didn't entirely get it either. The paradox is that the military trained strength into me yet expected complete compliance. Where was that balance? Why did I let it slide?

The fact was, I did my best not to think of it at all. It had been so long ago, but each time the topic reared its head, it felt brand new.

I knew I was destined to serve in the armed forces from childhood. There was never a question. Even had my parents not opted to tweak the embryo, they bled ARMY. I would surely follow in their footsteps. My parents carefully engineered their marriage around rank and duty station. It made perfect sense that they would plan for their only child to conform to those constraints.

Because of the genetic damage my mother had incurred during the Trusk wars, she and Dad were about to give up on parenthood. The doctors had informed them that conception would be questionable, and the likelihood of a healthy baby was doubtful. But then, the Soldier 2.0 program started, offering infertile service members a chance of parenthood with one caveat. Upon maturity, the service had dibs on the kid. So, instead of birthing babies, many folks were making GIs.

It wasn't like I had a lousy childhood. Quite the contrary, I got to see the world, meet different people, and absorb a wealth of diverse perspectives. It was a happy time. And to be honest, my military career had been vastly satisfying—until it wasn't.

Since my parents had instilled that strength of character when the recruiters came to visit, I held no hesitation or second thoughts. I was already basically living the life.

It was merely a matter of technicality. Since I was going in as a tweak, I didn't have to choose a MOS. My primary training would be targeted explicitly toward my abilities and leadership training. I excelled in the latter, but my abilities... well, I was a dud.

So, I spent most of my early career TDY. I'd be bounced from base to base on temporary assignments, one after another. I took that time to complete my education in engineering, learn about the inner workings of the ARMY, and even make some friends in the process. I studied everything the ARMY had to teach me. After some time, I had piled up enough points that my commanding officers recommended me for OCS.

Little did I know that my commission would be the beginning of the end.

I shook myself out of the memory. And for a moment, I was going to end the conversation, tell the girl to fuck off in new and creative ways. I was under no obligation to tell her anything. It was my business, my pain, my personal burden. I barely spoke to Al about it; he was as close as anyone had ever gotten to me. I opened my mouth to send her to hell. I tried, but it all spilled out.

"F...f...er... I was encouraged to begin a relationship with Major Everything, Nevin. They wanted to make more tweak kids to keep up appearances but preferred we made children the old-fashioned way."

"Why? There were tons of people willing to let their children be tweaked up."

Now, I was fully sucked into the conversation. Escape was impossible. "Yeah, but it was a different time. And they don't tell you that tweaking doesn't work as well as they claim."

"How do you mean? I'm okay."

"You're okay, but you're female. The problem is with the guys. They come out jacked up on power and aggression. You can't get one without the other. They've tried. Big power equals a big desire to dominate. Women come out stable and controllable but less powerful. And most of us are defensive. Subsequent generations have a better chance of being more powerful and stable. Second-gens have a decent likelihood of not going cray-cray. So, they figured they would pair me, a failed tweak with assumed dormant tweaks, with an ultra-powerful freak like Nevin and get a controllable superweapon."

"At least he was hot. You got along, right?"

I shook my head. "No. We did not."

"What was wrong with him? Everybody loved him."

"I didn't."

"Well, still, at least…"

"It's fucked up, and I don't want your fucking pity. So, drop it."

"Oh, you shut down." Om crossed her arms and took a smug stance. "I've seen this before in group."

"What the fuck does that mean?"

"Whatever super painful thing that happened to you, it makes you shut down emotionally. You repress everything and push people away."

"That's from your rehab group bullshit?"

"Yup." Om grinned. "Now, I get it. It's not pity, just understanding."

"Fuck off."

Om smiled. "Okay, you were forced into a shitty marriage to make a baby, and it sucked. How did that turn you into the Death Engine?"

"That." I sighed and clutched my head. "The tests showed the baby was substandard. The whole experiment was a freaking failure. Then, there were Nevin's extracurricular outings and the oversight hearings. They covered up a lot of shit. You couldn't imagine."

"Didn't some bad guy firebomb your house?"

"Some bad guy, yeah. Nexum decided to wipe the slate clean in response to public backlash against human DNA tweaking. All those government contractors were taking heat for their folly and needed to get rid of the evidence. It didn't help that Nevin was completely out of control, and they were having trouble keeping it out of the media. They hit us with the only thing that could take Nevin out: extreme combustion. I wasn't supposed to walk away. They spun it as a terrorist attack on two cherished heroes. When Nexum came to clean up the debris and found me regenerating, they counted themselves lucky."

"Holy crap, no wonder you're a dysfunctional bitch."

"Fuck you, you little shit. You have a mental tweak. Don't you? That's how you made me spill my guts."

Om shrugged. "I can't help it if people find it easy to talk to me. Besides, you needed to let it out."

"So, you're spying for Fuckmuffin?"

"Nope." Om shook her head. "He doesn't know about my special skill. All that is between us."

"Well, fuck you anyway."

"You already said that, like fifty-seven times."

"You don't listen," I replied.

"I listen. I don't obey. I'm not a good follower. That's why the military chose to cancel the contract. Well, that and the drugs."

"That would do it." I snickered. "Nice job. You're a fucked-up mess too."

"Oh, I am, but not as screwed up as you. And I'm clean now."

"You seem to be glued back together, okay," I said. "But you know, you may slip. It happens."

"I know. And you may go on a psycho killing spree."

I shrugged. "Maybe"

Om held out her hand. "Friends?"

"Something, I dunno." I shook her hand. "But don't tell anyone. They'll only screw with you."

"It's cool," Om replied. "Thanks."

"Guess we have to get back to Fuckdog."

"Yup."

We arrived at the training area as Keen demonstrated hand-to-hand techniques to the boys. Purple Flame had a far better grip on self-defense than I would have expected. He needed work, but he appeared competent enough.

"Eris," Keen bellowed. "Nice to have you join us."

"I would have been here sooner had you not killed me."

"True. We're going to move on and practice some basic martial arts techniques. Why don't you come let me demonstrate?"

"Okay." I stepped up to face Keen. He threw a punch. I tried redirecting it, but my arm was much slower than expected. It was all the added weight of the armor power. Keen connected, but I felt nothing. He winced and quickly pulled back his hand.

"You're slow," he pointed out.

"I know. For some reason, my body is really heavy now. I'm trying to adjust."

"Hit the weights and the speed bag for now. We'll use this to our advantage. When the power wears off, your arm will feel lighter. You should be faster than before."

"Okay." I nodded and went over to the weight bench to begin working out. I watched him with the kids as I trained. His lessons weren't bad, but something didn't sit well with me. It felt like his heart wasn't into it. Like he was only doing it as a show of effort, not to achieve any results. He wasn't letting the kids practice anything for any significant length of time. Fucknuts only showed them a move once or twice before moving on to the next thing. It wasn't even close enough to the repetition and practice needed for muscle memory or to develop basic understanding. Nor did he encourage them to take notes. And when they did something wrong, he barely made the effort to correct them.

Maybe I was overreacting. The kids were picking up some of the training despite the lack of practice. So, maybe my paranoia was just that. Perhaps this was Fuckburger's way of teaching. By the end of the day, the kids were far more confident in themselves as a team than when they started, which was definite progress.

After practice, I grabbed my stuff and took a bus to Al's house. Luckily, the driver didn't notice the sagging in the suspension caused by my excessive weight.

The front door opened for me as I approached. A small piece of Al managed the house and recognized me. It turned the lights on to a comfortable level and adjusted the air temperature.

Pictures of a happy Ji-hoon and Boy were sprinkled around the house. Their images smiled warm memories onto the house. It felt like a home, even if it wasn't mine.

I missed my little retirement trailer, but it was never completely a home, even with the cat and the neighbors. I hadn't had a real home since I joined the military as a teenager. Until this point, I hadn't realized how much it bothered me. Being in Al's house stirred up more of the emotional debris I had long ago sunk below my consciousness. I contemplated leaving, ditching all this sentiment, and shutting out the pain. Instead, I stripped down to my underwear and collapsed onto the sofa. I passed out immediately.

The dreams kicked in again. But my exhaustion was extreme enough to keep me under. Like sleeping through leg cramps, my body and mind accepted the pain but slid past it, allowing me to slumber.

When I awoke, I found myself under a pile of blankets. The smell of coffee wafted in. I sat up and realized I was no longer on the sofa but in the master bedroom.

"Hey, why'd you move me?" I yelled.

"It appears that you've gained substantial weight since yesterday," Al shouted from the kitchen. "You were damaging my sofa. My bed is reinforced enough to handle several tons."

"Oh, sorry."

"Want to talk about it?" Al walked into the room and handed me a mug of coffee. "Did you sleep okay?"

"Eh, actually, I slept better than expected. Fuckturd shot me in the head yesterday to make a point."

"That he is an asshole?"

"Yeah," I laughed. "That, and I was late. He was training some children. Their shock almost made it worthwhile."

"Why are you even giving him your time?"

"It's not like I have a choice. Someone took me out of retirement to work with the fucker. I'll never find out what's going on if I don't play along. What else can I do?"

"Run away."

"I keep trying that." I sighed and clutched my temples. "It hasn't been working out."

Al sat on the bed next to me. "Run. I can hide you."

"No, you can't. I did a perfect job this last time. Whoever sent RoboBash found me, anyway."

"You shouldn't be doing this again."

"I know, but I have no other ideas. I'll do this one and find an escape plan before they weaponise me again."

"I don't approve of this plan."

"Thank you," I smirked.

"For what? Disapproving?"

"No, for caring."

He leaned in. "I will always care."

"I know. You're the only one who ever did."

"Not even your family?"

"My family has been dead for a long time. You're it."

"You're complicated," he said. "Like me."

"Yeah, but around you, I almost feel almost normal. I can talk to you."

Al reached out to touch me but then pulled back. "I have to go do inventory at the bar. Meet me there later?"

"Yeah."

Al took off. I got dressed and went to training.

Chapter 4

Another day of practice passed without my death. I was feeling pretty good about it. At the end of the day, I walked over to Spaz for a celebratory drink and good company. That's when the YouHump truck almost ran me over. Before I could open my mouth to curse out the driver, I was struck again by the realization. The block was nearly empty. Most of the houses were dark and empty. It was like a ghost town.

"Where did they all go?" I asked myself out loud.

"Gone," a voice said. "Like you should be."

"Says who?" I asked.

"Says the one holding the gun. Give me your wallet."

I laughed.

"I'm not joking." My assailant was a twenty-something loser in knock-off, overpriced, fad wear. The clothes were the wrong size, half too tight, the other half significantly too loose. It was apparent they were stolen. He held a firearm poorly.

"So, you ever going to clean that weapon?" I asked. "It looks like you wiped your ass with it."

"Screw the gun," he said. "I didn't ask you about that shit. I told you to give me your money."

"No, you didn't, fucktard."

"What did you just say?" He twitched.

"I said you didn't tell me that. You told me to give you my wallet. You never fucking said anything about money. I also called you a fucktard. But I was wrong, you're not a fucktard."

"That's right," he said. "You take that back. Now give me the money and wallet."

"Nope. You're worse than a fucktard."

"What, are you insane? I will shoot you." He pointed the gun at my head.

"No, you won't. You know why?"

"There's no *why*. I'm about to pull the trigger. I'll shoot you in the head."

"You can't do it. You're too much of a pussy."

I could practically hear the gears in his head grind to a halt as his brain tried to process the absolute heinousness of my response.

"That's it, you're toast!" He jerked up his elbow and pointed the gun in a weird, cartoon-like angle at my face.

"Yeah, give me that." I stepped forward and sidestepped the barrel of the gun. Then, I simply yanked the weapon out of his hands. "Now, give me your wallet."

He stood there, unmoving. I reached into his back pocket and removed his wallet.

"Go home," I barked. "Before I make you fire this shit and blow your own fucking face off."

The guy took off like an asshat in the night.

"You should come around more often. That idiot has lots of friends I'd like to see... go away."

I turned to see an old man walking his dog.

"They've been preying on us for a while. That's why everyone is moving to Mars, or the outer colonies, anywhere but Earth."

"What about the cops?"

"Cops." He shook his head. "Have you been living under a rock? Cops have been gone for years. We're on our own. That's why everyone is leaving. The colonies are cheap, and the violence here is high. I only hope it gets quiet again after they all leave."

"I had no idea," I said. "I was retired at Champion Acres."

"That explains the cocky attitude," he replied. "Should I know you?"

"Nope."

"You look young for the memory ward."

"Looks can be deceiving," I replied. "I've seen some shit."

The man nodded. "I believe it."

"So, it's been that bad?"

"Yeah," he answered. "The jobs started to dry up. Then, nobody had money to spend, and all the local businesses closed. Crime went up. Then, a few years ago, people started running. It started as a trickle, but it snowballed. Better paying jobs, better housing out there." He pointed at the sky. "They even sponsor minimum wage workers to go to the outer colonies. It's hard to resist."

"You did."

"This is my home. I'm comfortable here."

"I get it. Sometimes, you want to plant roots."

"Exactly."

"I tried that a few times. Didn't stick."

"Maybe it will next time," he said.

"Don't know." I shrugged. "I kind of like it here. Full of fucktardtainment. Oh, here." I threw him the wallet. "Maybe there's something in there to make up for that asshat's past bullshit."

He stuck the wallet in his jacket pocket. "I'll put it to good use."

"Someone decent should."

"Thank you, young lady." He tipped his hat. "Have a lovely evening."

I arrived at Spaz to find mayhem. Immediately, I was assaulted by the sounds of shouting and crashing. I first noticed Al on the floor with a man swinging a large crowbar at his leg. Two other men smashed the place with bats. I ran and dived into Al's assailant. We tumbled to the floor, neither of us gaining an advantage. He swung a punch, striking me in my upper hip, barely missing my ribcage. We both scrambled to our feet, but I was quicker. I kicked him in the skull, and he fell back to the floor. I kicked him several more times in his head and body to make sure he learned something. This drew the attention of the other two morons.

They charged me. One head-butted me in the midsection, but I was too angry to go down. Instead of falling, the inertia flung us backward into a table. I rolled to my right side, causing us to bounce off a chair and land on the ground. This time, I was on top. I brutally pounded the man's midsection. When I felt his ribs crack, I knew he wasn't getting up anytime soon. I halted my attack in time to see the third man run out the door. I apprehensively let him go. I wanted to give him chase, but there were more pressing issues to deal with.

"How the hell did you survive these years without me?" I snapped.

"I've been fine," Al replied.

"You can't fight your way out of a paper bag. I'm surprised you faked it for this long."

"I can fight. I choose not to."

"Yeah, I can see that." I offered my hand to Al. He took it, and I pulled him to his feet. "So, what happened?"

"There was a disagreement," Al replied.

"There's always a disagreement. Did those douchebags damage you?"

"No, no damage." Al took a step and stumbled. "It's nothing."

"You're limping."

"No."

"Al."

"Maybe they hit me once or twice."

"Maybe? With that crowbar?"

Al just grunted.

"And what were you fighting about?" I asked.

"The gentlemen wanted to buy the bar from me and offered a large sum, but I told them I wasn't interested. They didn't want to take no for an answer and stated that the neighborhood was in decline. They suggested I reconsider. When I would not, they decided to demonstrate why it was dangerous here."

"Well, we educated them."

"Yes," Al replied. "They learned a painful lesson."

"Let me see the leg."

"No, I'm fine."

"You keep saying that. I don't think you know what 'fine' means."

"It means I am uninjured."

"Al, stop being a fucktard, get in your office."

"Yes, Eris." Al limped into his office, and I followed. I closed the door behind us and gathered the tools.

"Okay, drop 'em," I said.

"That's what she said."

"Really? You're sinking down to my level."

"Yes."

"Sit down and let me see the leg."

Al sat in his chair.

"This is a mess," I said. The leg was bent in two places from what looked like previous damage. "Have you been doing your own repairs?"

"Who else would do it?" Al asked.

"Well, you're being sloppy. Wait, is this supposed to be some kind of splint you welded in here?"

Al tried to stand up and walk away. I pushed him back down.

"Sit and be still. I'll fix what I can so you can walk."

I pulled out the magnifying goggles and the nano soldering station and got to work.

Al shifted in his chair, and I nearly took out a sensor with the soldering iron.

"I said be still," I smacked his good leg. "I almost took out one of the fifty million sensors in the leg. Who uses this many?"

"Ji-hoon got sensor-happy," Al replied. "As he got older, he started installing them every time he made any type of repair. I asked him to refrain, but he insisted that I would need them someday. It became uncomfortable to move around."

"Why so many sensors? Redundancy?"

"I would rather not say."

"Rather not say?" I paused when it hit me. "Oh."

"He thought I might need companionship one day."

"Damn, Ji-hoon was a dirty old man."

"Yes, he was. But he sensed his own mortality and didn't want me to be alone. After you and I met, he continually asked if I banged you yet."

I laughed. "Ji-hoon obviously didn't know me."

"Obviously," Al replied.

"You ever try them out?"

"No," Al scoffed indignantly. "Who would I test them with?"

"You know, when you're home alone, you could put on some soft music, dim the lights, and start playing with sensors."

"I have more valuable things to do with my time."

"I could build you something." I grinned. "You know, a sensor-toy."

"No."

"Come on! You need to run diagnostics on them somehow. You might as well enjoy it."

"I can run diagnostics just fine without special tools."

I shook my head. "You are the definition of uptight."

"And you're not?"

"I'm not…shut the fuck up." I finished the last connection. "There, better?"

"Yes, much."

"You need another leg," I said. "You have serious metal fatigue here."

"I don't want a new one," Al said.

"You have no choice," I replied. "If you are so attached to this one, you can put it in a drawer as a keepsake, but you're not walking on this shit anymore."

"Parts are costly."

"Bullshit," I said. "You said that parts are easy to come by."

"Easy to come by, but not cheap," Al retorted.

"I'll cover it. I'll be back with a leg."

"No," Al objected.

"Do you really think you can stop me?"

Al didn't answer.

"I'll be back soon. And stop pouting."

"I'm not pouting."

"Are too." I closed the door behind me before he got the last word.

I walked across town to Raylene's Robotics and Electronics. To say that the building was dilapidated would have been an understatement. Deathtrap was a better description. The sign hung precariously from the left corner like it would fall at any moment. Half of the windows were boarded up, planks covered holes in the floor, and several buckets were scattered around the room to catch water from the leaky roof. The lighting was dim, making it hard to see the inventory.

I was about to pull off my sunglasses when I saw the shrine. In the corner of the store, a small alcove was carved out. No merchandise was displayed in the area, only a tribute to the tweak heroes of all time. "Fuck me," I muttered.

A poster of the Peace League hung in the center encased in plastic. I gazed at it in disgust.

There I was, with my pink-pixie hair, clad in spandex and dreams. The costume was a little more high-tech than spandex, but it was stretchy and highlighted my handler's favorite parts.

Major Everything stood next to me. Well, no. I was standing next to Major Everything, not the other way around. I hung just an inch back to demonstrate that he was in charge and that I was his faithful girl.

A surge of hatred shot through my chest. I was glad he was dead. I even caught myself grinning. Things might have been different if not for him. I could have been happy. And I had been—until—

I remember the day so clearly. I had barely stepped off the plane from Greenland when I was intercepted by a flock of brass and contractors. Two of them were grinning and staring directly at my chest.

"Captain Eris? Would you please join us? We're taking you to your next assignment." I don't remember which of the sleazoids spoke first, but I was whisked onto another plane before I knew it.

One of the contractors took over my briefing. He was in a dark blue suit, generic looking, and called himself 'Bob.'

"Captain, we've come to understand that you've performed exemplary in a number of assignments. You have the reputation of being reliable and even heroic. To be honest, you are an untapped resource, a diamond in the rough. The PR you could generate is incredible. So you have been selected."

"I'm sorry, Bob." I remember being completely taken aback. "Selected for what?"

"We're forming a team of sorts, and your skills and accomplishments make you ideal for it."

"And you jiggle well." Another suit named 'Gene' giggled off to the side.

"Wait, what?" I didn't like where this was going.

"Trust me, you're perfect." Bob slapped my knee. "You're going to be a superhero."

The shock struck me like a lead weight. How was I, a powerless tweak-failure, going to be a superhero?

"I, uh, is this an order?"

"Absolutely," Bob answered. "I have the paperwork right here." He patted his briefcase.

When I arrived at my new assignment, my stomach turned. The place was packed with costumed douche-bros who stared at my ass like I was the evening's meal.

My barracks were simultaneously sparse and extravagant. I had no dresser, closet or bathroom door, but there was a complete entertainment system and a queen-sized bed. Once I was given my assignments, it started to make more sense.

From day one, my meals were regulated to the crumb. I wasn't permitted to gain even one extra pound, even if that meant starving me for a day or two. I'd never had a weight problem, nor did I pay any mind to my mass. I was fit and strong, which is all the bastards should have cared about. But now they were harping on about waist sizes and hip measurements.

For the first month I was on base, I was measured, critiqued, and made over.

My uniform was replaced with spandex. My boots were substituted with heels. A push-up bra was added to my 'uniform.' There were distinct orders that I should never be in any shoes with heels under four inches. I had to learn to run, fight, and dance in them, all while being ogled by different company men.

I hardly spoke to anyone during those days. That was until I was introduced to the team. And yes, it was a small pack of costumed douche-bros, and they were betting on who would "split me in two" first.

But the humiliation was just beginning. Soon, the spandex started getting scantier, the heels higher, and the evaluations more physically intrusive.

And then they did the unthinkable. They colored my hair cotton candy pink. It was ghastly.

That's when I was introduced to our assigned contracting company, Nexum. And boy, did they have plans for me.

They spun me as a superpowered national hero, strong, confident, and packed into a kicking body. The thing was, I didn't feel like any of that. Before the transformation, I was mighty, unstoppable, but once the costume crap began, I just felt ridiculous. Even all these years later, that feeling never went away.

I growled, clenching my fists in anger and embarrassment. Despite the passage of time, it still felt raw. I should never have let them, never—

"What do you need?" An overweight twenty-something in an anime t-shirt appeared from the back and slid behind the counter.

I took a moment to rebalance and approached him. "Yeah, I have a list of parts. Can I send them to your invebase?"

"Do you think this is a Smart Purchase or something?"

"Okay, do you have anything I can write on?"

"Why?" he asked.

"So, I can give you a list of what I need."

"Everything's out there." He motioned to the rows of bins and shelves that filled the space.

"Great. Could you turn up the lights a little?"

"You could just take off your sunglasses."

"Yeah." I spun around and removed my sunglasses, making sure the guy wasn't looking at my face. I sorted through bins and shelves, rummaging through outdated and used parts.

"You have anything a little less ancient?" I asked.

"People who want new stuff don't come here."

"Yeah," I grumbled and continued the search. After about an hour, I found three acceptable limbs that could be combined to work. I brought them to the counter to pay for them.

"Planning to build something heavy-duty, I see." He examined the components.

"Yup. Something huge."

The guy tallied up the charges and handed me the itemized list. It was pricey but reasonable. I gave him a stack of coin cards.

"Thanks." He looked up at me. "Wait, aren't you?"

Sunglasses. I forgot to put the fucking sunglasses back on.

"I'm nobody."

"No, you used to be her." He pointed at the poster of the Peace League encased within the shrine.

"How would that be possible? Wouldn't she be well over a hundred-fifty by now?"

"I don't know. But you're a dead ringer, besides the uniform and the hair color."

"Lucky me. I look like a perky pop tweak."

"She didn't stay perky," the guy dropped his voice to a near whisper. "She became very dark after mercenaries killed her husband and almost killed her. She went on a bloody rampage and disappeared. Some people say she's still out there. They say she's immortal and plotting vengeance to this day."

I felt like yelling 'Boo!' but thought better of it. I had more important things to deal with. "Do you believe that?"

"I don't know." He shrugged. "I like to hope Captain Eris found peace. She did good stuff before they hurt her."

"Or maybe she's still out there, plotting." I grinned.

"If so, someone's in big trouble. I wouldn't want to get on her bad side." He put my items in a box.

"Thanks." I grabbed the box. "Have a nice day."

"You, too. Come back anytime."

I took public transit to Al's place to drop off the parts. The faces of the passengers, beaten, tired, and bleak, were disheartening. The vehicle was deceptively full. The city had reduced the transport frequency to compensate for the dwindling population. It felt like I was living in a dying world, like we were the last remnants of an extinct species. The sensation was suffocating and hollow. I wanted to stop, fade into the universe, and become something else.

Once at my stop, I stepped onto the street and absorbed the madness of it all. The entire world is being replaced by an upgrade. It set off my 'this is gonna be shit' alarm.

Dropping my packages in the house, I took a moment and breathed in the ghost of Ji-hoon, silently vowing to watch over his neglected son. Al was letting himself go to hell, and I had to intervene. It was going to be a long, late night of arguing and cleaning.

I went out again, walking to the hardware store. It was still early, yet I hadn't encountered a single soul. When I entered Krish's Hardware, I was the only patron. The owner, Krish, sat at the front counter. A picture of his younger self and his family hung on the wall behind him. The history of Krish's better days plastered the space. All the standard tropes were there. Their first cashcoin, business and insurance certificates, and more images of patrons, relatives, and friends. He had a vacant look in his eyes.

"Hello," I greeted.

"Hi," Krish answered.

"Busy day?" I grabbed a basket and began filling it with miscellaneous items.

"It is now," he answered. "No people, no customers."

"You're still here."

"Terminal cancer. Pointless to go anywhere. Family is gone. Store is all I got."

"Oh." I was at a loss for words. "Sorry."

"It's alright. I accepted my fate. Have you accepted yours?"

"That's an odd question. But no." I shook my head. "I battle my fate every day."

"Seems like a terrible waste of energy."

"It is what it is. It's my way." I put my basket on the counter and reached into my pocket.

"Don't bother," he said. "It's not going to matter in a few weeks."

"It matters to me." I dropped a pile of cash coins on the counter. "Do something fun. Don't go out with regrets."

He smiled. "I have no regrets. I've lived my life." He took the money off the counter. "But I'll be happy to oblige you. Have a little fun."

I forced a smile. "Good."

Walking out of the door, I felt emptier than before and wondered how much worse I could feel. I grabbed some takeout on the way back to the house. Fortunately, the Chinese takeout place was not a complete downer. In the restaurant trade, being morose could be bad for business.

Al got home early. He wasn't walking well.

"Early close?" I asked.

"It was dead," he replied. "The regulars went home. There was no point in staying open."

"Good, because it's time to get naked in the garage."

Al looked around at the bags and boxes of parts.

"What's your plan?" he asked suspiciously.

"We're going to rebuild the leg and do a full tune-up."

"I'm not comfortable with that."

"Fuck you. Get in the garage."

"Cursing will not change my mind."

"I *will* repair you, even if I have to tie you down." I stepped up to him until I was on my tippy toes and centimeters from his face. "Try me."

We stood deadlocked for some time.

"Fine." Al walked into the garage and took off his clothes. "Proceed."

I set up a bunch of old-school halogen lights but left all of them off except one for the time being. They were hot, which I would need later. I started with the leg. It took several hours just to get all the components to work together. Moving around all the sensory components and adjusting them all took even more time. Next, I moved on to the tune-up.

"You're a freaking mess," I complained.

"Am not," Al replied.

"You're also a fucking liar."

"Your vocabulary is filthy," he stated.

"Your personal hygiene is worse."

Al grunted in objection.

I replaced the bad cables and relays, cleaning everything that could be cleaned. I tested and documented each component within reason and even reverse-engineered Ji-hoon's pervy sensor array.

"Impressive." I examined the components with a probe. "These pathways were originally designed as a feedback mechanism for a targeting system. Ji-hoon repurposed it to trigger positive feedback when the ideal stimulus is detected. Shit, some of these things even have haptic feedback. Incredible."

"He was very hedonistic."

I nodded. "Yeah, but the way this is designed, painstakingly. He really cared about you getting laid."

"I dread to consider how he came by the data to program the optimal stimulus."

I laughed. "We may never know. But that explains why you can't fight. All your combat systems are dedicated to pleasing the ladies. Unless you don't swing that way."

"I can fight. And I don't swing, anyway."

"Bullshit. Well, you're almost done here. You're reset to optimal functionality. At least your body is. You're on your own with the cognitive shit. Stay put." I broke out a can of paint and shook it up.

"What's that?" he asked.

"Gunmetal gray. It will be a good look for you. Very sexy and mysterious."

"It's late."

"Eh," I looked at the time. "Only 4 a.m."

"I didn't agree to a paint job."

"We need to protect the metal, fartknocker."

"I now question your maturity level," Al said.

"Only just now? It took all these years to notice that... Mr. *That's-What-She-Said.*"

I started from his feet and worked my way up. Typically, I would have done it top-down, but since he was being whiny, I wanted to work on his face last. It was making a huge difference. He looked clean and pulled together.

I broke out the airbrush and filled it. Then, I took some tape and covered one of Al's eyes. I began painting the side of his face.

He grabbed my arm with his sticky hand. "Be careful!"

"Don't worry. I won't damage the merchandise."

I finished his head and checked the body for drips, orange peeling or missed spots.

It was 7 a.m. before I was satisfied with my work.

"Looking good." I nodded. "You look years younger."

"Thank you."

"You're welcome." I turned on all the lights and adjusted them to point directly at him. "I have to go to work. You stand here perfectly still until you have to leave. The paint needs to set."

"What?" he yelled. "Eris!"

"Don't move," I shouted as I ran out of the house.

"What is that stench?" Om waved her hand in front of her face.

"That is the smell of paint and desperation." I sat next to her on a bench against the gym wall.

"What?"

"Never mind." I cracked open a bottle of water and chugged it. I still felt dehydrated.

"You look like hell."

"I was up all night helping a friend."

"You have friends?"

"You're a fucking comedian." I pulled out an energy bar and forced it down. "Okay, watch Bushysan."

"Yeah?"

"See how he's stiff and rigid in his movements, yet he's somehow sloppy about it."

"Yeah, I see it," Om replied.

"That's what a cheap strip mall black belt looks like. And Bushysan has the douchebag personality to go with it."

Om giggled.

"I'm completely serious. You have to learn these things. This way, you know who you're fighting. I'm not a great fighter. The dying thing aside, I have some basic training, but my skills are mediocre at best. What I'm good at is knowing my enemy. You don't need to throw the best punch in the world. You just need to know where to land your shitty punch. It also helps if you can psych them out. That's why I talk shit during a fight."

"I thought you did it to be funny."

"Well, it does amuse me. But it serves the purpose of distracting my opponent. Sometimes, it backfires, and they hit me harder. In my case, that's okay. You may not want to do that. You can try it on, but if it doesn't fit, don't taunt."

"Okay." Om nodded.

"See Purple Flame? He's clumsy, but he's not stiff. He doesn't know how to fight. He's been faking it. But he's cool. We don't want to smack him. If we did, I'd take him out by his legs. He is a bench presser. He works his upper body and neglects his lower body entirely. See the imbalance?"

"I see. That's why Flame's so dorky—it's messing with his balance."

"You got it. All you need to do is practice the basics and know your enemy. Do whatever Keen teaches you in training, but focus on the basics at home. Low kicks, strategically placed punches, and not being there when someone attacks."

"Got it."

"Good." I crunched up the energy bar wrapper and shoved it in my pocket. "You will get hit, but you have a much better chance of winning if you keep a clear head. So don't freak out if someone connects. Control your heart rate. If you remain calm during the fight, you will win. Can you do those things?"

Om nodded again. "Yes, I can."

"Then you will be fine."

"I'll live, but I'm not sure if I will be fine."

"Why," I asked. "What's bothering you?"

"I don't know. I guess I'm feeling a little disillusioned."

"About what?"

"I wanted to, you know, join a super team and save the world. I wanted to be part of something bigger—feel like I belonged. This is okay, but it doesn't feel like I thought it would."

"This situation is not ideal," I said. "You'll find your team one day."

"I should have stayed clean and joined the service."

"What, and end up with pink hair, a spandex mini dress, performing in video remakes of classical pop? Nah, you're doing it right. Do your own thing and make your own choices. You're doing great."

"Really?"

"Yeah. Absolutely. You're okay."

"Thanks," Om replied. "I think I feel better."

"Good, let's go screw with the boys."

Keen gave us a day off, and I decided to make the best of it. I sat in Al's recliner, drank beer, and watched Xtreme sports on vid. I was comfortable, almost relaxed. I would have the house to myself all day, so I was blissfully slobbed out. My hair was uncombed, and I was in my underwear. It was a luxury I had not enjoyed for weeks. It was glorious.

A rocket boarding competition was airing. Jucan Paulie, the leading champion, was competing against Angroz Newak. Newak was making a surprising showing. His tricks were more complex than the judges expected. He scored very well. Jucan was going to have to bring his A-game. Jucan took his place on the lip of the hyperpipe. He kicked off and…

There was a knock on the door. I didn't respond.

I turned my attention to Jucan and his run. His tricks were excellent, but it would be close. The judges awarded him a nearly perfect score. The match was nearly tied. The next run would determine the contest.

The knock returned.

"Go away," I yelled.

The knocking became more insistent. Then, it turned into a pounding.

"Motherfucker!" I cursed, hoping that they heard me. I threw the door open. "What?"

"Good morning." A woman in a maroon blazer and matching slacks stood before me. "I represent DoLess Realty. Did you know your neighbors sold their homes for a substantial profit?"

"I don't care! Fuck off."

"You could make a substantial profit. With that, you could buy a mansion on the outer planets or even a condo on Mars."

"Did you not hear me the first time?" I asked. "I'm not interested. Fuck off."

"Let me give you a brochure. It will show you some options and the advantages of off-world living."

"Take that brochure and shove it up your twat, you cum bag. Is that clear enough?" I slammed the door in her smug realtor face and went back to rocket boarding.

Just as I sat, the knocking started again.

I opened the door. Now, a man stood at the door. He was dressed in the same uniform style as the woman.

"You upset my colleague," he stated. "Perhaps you didn't understand the amazing deal she was offering you."

"I don't fucking care." I assumed a fight stance, hoping he'd catch on to his impending danger. "Go the fuck away. Don't make me say it again."

"If I could just give you this brochure—"

"If you knock one more time, I will beat you until you have to use your brochures to stop the bleeding. Go away." I slammed the door.

They knocked again. I didn't answer. I turned the volume up to drown them out. It was just starting to work when the commercial break cut in.

"Life on Earth got you down?" A man appeared with his face in his hands. Around him, images of crime, bill collection notices, an angry spouse and crying children appeared. *"Ever dream of a Mars lifestyle, but you*

simply don't have the resources? Then the Outer Colonies are for you!" Images of luxury living swirled into view. Smiling faces replaced the sad ones. *"Call your local real estate professional and see how we can make your dream lifestyle a reality!"*

At that moment, I knew I would fail to recover my moment of peace.

I got dressed to go out. When I opened the front door, I was assaulted by a meter-high pile of brochures. "Damn it!" I screamed to the sky.

I wandered downtown to do a little window shopping. The streets were spotless but practically abandoned. A few older people shuffled along the sidewalks. They looked up at the sky, watching freighter after freighter escaping Earth's atmosphere. I could almost feel the ships fighting the grip of the planet, struggling to break free from its clingy grasp as if the planet itself was imploring its inhabitants to stay. I felt a pang of longing for the world of the past. Despite its sometimes hostile nature, it was at least alive.

I gave up and dragged myself back to the bar. Thankfully, the place was hopping. I needed the sounds of humanity to displace the deafening silence.

"Al, give me something strong." I threw myself onto a bar stool.

"I thought you were relaxing at home."

"The damn real estate agents kept fucking with me. Harshed my entire day."

"Yes. They've been increasingly aggressive."

I held up a clenched fist. "I want to strangle them."

Al handed me a shot. I drank it.

"Why don't they go away?" I asked.

"I suppose they have to make a living."

"Well, no means no."

George walked in. He tried to avoid eye contact with me. He walked up to the bar. "Give me a whiskey."

"Yo, George, we cool?"

George nodded. "We're good."

"Sorry, I hit you."

"Sorry, I called you a slut."

"It's cool," I said. "I noticed you've been hitting it hard lately."

"I've had a shit time." He threw back his shot.

"Been there. It doesn't end well. Give yourself and your liver a break. Really. No bitch is worth it."

"You seem okay."

"Do I?" I asked. "Do I really seem okay?"

George shrugged. "You're breathing."

"I'm always breathing. It doesn't mean much."

"What else can I do? Years of marriage gone." George held up the glass. "This is the only thing that dulls the pain."

"Maybe you shouldn't dull it. Maybe you need to feel the pain so you can work through it."

"Sounds like touchy, feely, new age bullshit to me."

"Maybe, but it's better than the nuclear option. The booze will kill you. But it's all on you if you want to let *her* win."

"She already won," George complained. "She left me with nothing but misery. May as well drown my sorrows."

"Listen, I drank myself to death once, cirrhosis of the liver. It took a few years. It was a painful death, and I felt every second of it. It happens like that. You get to the point that you know it's killing you, but you can't stop. The worst part of it for me was when I came back. I couldn't even drown my sorrows because I was immune. But you won't come back, so it doesn't matter, I guess. I mean, if you want to fucking die, go ahead. But you may want to pick a less painful method."

George looked at me and sighed. "I don't know what else to do."

"I don't know, go to the gym. Take up the violin. Ask Sam for a brutal job and beat it out on someone else. Use your pain for something constructive. Don't just curl up in a ball and die. It's pathetic."

George nodded. "Okay, I'll try to ease up. Thanks." He held out his hand.

I shook it. "No worries."

After a couple of hours of listening to George whining about his ho-hopper soon-to-be ex-wife, I needed a breath of non-tweak space. There weren't many options available after ten o'clock on a weekday, so corporate-branded coffee was it was.

I popped in and ordered a triple espresso shot, because fuck sleep. As I sat and waited, watching the line of pencil-necked Doomers ordering their 12-ingredient chemical motivation, I caught sight of a familiar purple mohawk moving behind the counter. I popped over and waved.

Purple Flame practically jumped into the back shelf.

"Sorry." I grinned. "Shitty day job. I get it."

Purple Flame shook himself out of his shock. "Yeah. I have a kid."

"Ah," I nodded. "Didn't mean to catch you mid secret identity."

Flame grinned and shook his head. "I'm not much of a hero. I did some time and you know."

"You're working a crap corp job. You're a hero. I can't do that."

"Yeah, well, you're insane." Flame looked around.

"Don't worry, I'm outie as soon as I get my caffeine."

"It's cool." Purple Flame ran his hand through his hair. "I just don't want to blow this, you know, but I need money for the kid. And there aren't a lot of quick ways Yes." I sighed. "I plan to stay..." to, um, get it."

I nodded. "Rock and a hard place. I—"

"—order for Felch M...Ew!"

"That's me." I grinned. "See you later PF." With that, I turned and grabbed my coffee from the counter and headed home.

Stepping through the door, I was greeted by the sounds of domestication.

"Take my bed." Al exited the kitchen where he had been stocking up groceries for me.

"The couch is fine." I stripped down to my underwear and started to sit on the sofa.

Al grabbed my arm to stop me. "Please don't."

His grip was gentle but firm, oddly not unpleasant. "Okay. I can always sleep in the guest room."

"No, that's for guests. You're not a guest."

"Al, you know that makes no freaking sense."

"It does to me. You have a tendency to gain weight. I don't want you destroying the furniture."

"I'm okay now. What the hell?"

"I don't want you to get into any bad habits."

"Bad habits? Really? Okay, aibee, where will you sleep then?"

"I don't need to sleep." He looked away, avoiding eye contact.

"You need to backup, it's the same freaking thing. What's this really about?"

"I want you to be comfortable. The sofa is not comfortable."

"And the bed in the guest room is made of rocks? Are you just looking for ways to get me into your bed? Trying to get lucky tonight?"

Al grunted. "Stay on the sofa. Suit yourself."

"Wait, just tell me why."

"I prefer knowing where you are… in case."

"In case what? In case someone breaks in? In case of fire?"

Al just gazed at me.

"Oh, you're afraid I'm going to kill myself when you're offline." I sighed. "Why the sudden concern?"

"It's not sudden. You're always plotting your own demise."

"Not always. Just on the bad days."

"You have many of those."

"And you can watch me better in your bedroom?"

"I can monitor my room while offline to stay protected during vulnerable times."

"What if I promise not to attempt suicide for a while?"

"Define a while."

"Okay." I threw my arms up in the air. "I'll sleep where you can watch me. Wait, does this mean you watch me everywhere I go?"

"I respect your privacy," he replied.

"But?"

"I may occasionally search for your vitals throughout the day."

"You know that's creepy shit, verging on stalking."

"It isn't intended as such."

"I know. That's why I'm not going to punch you. You've been lonely, haven't you?"

Al nodded. "I have."

"Okay, I'll take your bed, and I promise not to kill myself intentionally. But could you keep the creepy stalking thing to a minimum?"

Al put his hand on my shoulder. "I promise."

When I entered the room, I grinned at its orderliness. It reminded me of my old BAH. Even when I lived out in the economy, I liked things tidy.

I took my armful of clothes and walked into the closet. There were several empty hangers available to me. I grabbed a couple and stashed my gear.

There were other outfits there, some that Al wore to appear more human, a few trendy items that I could only assume once belonged to Boy, and, oddly, something more familiar. Bloodstained and torn, my old Death

Engine suit hung like a testimony to my immortality. I opened my mouth to call Al but thought better of it.

I pulled it off the hanger and examined every millimeter. It wasn't pink and perky like my Peace League uniform. It was a heavy green and black, angry garment. The knife hole only accentuated the violence the suit had endured.

The stabbing occurred the last time I'd worked with Keen. I was dropped into the action as insurance. Nexum was making a deal with some super sketchy operatives from another contractor. I didn't know the details. I was just a body, a deterrent.

When things went sideways, a lot of people died. I had taken most of them down. But the action was too loud and public. I had to dig in—find a quiet, fortified spot. I ducked into a tweak bar, looking to hide among the other costumed freaks. But that action wasn't sanctioned. So, I found myself on the other end of friendly fire - well, friendly stabbing, to be more specific - on the way through the door. I didn't see my assailant, but I always suspected Keen. He was duplicitous and loved edged weapons. He got me good. I had barely made it into the bathroom before I died. Before Al found me.

I clutched the fabric to my chest and felt the tears falling down my cheek. Freaking Al.

Chapter 5

The decorative hedge beside the makeshift target burst into flame.

"No." I grabbed Om's wrist and shook it. "Why the hell are you jerking your arm up before you squeeze the trigger?"

"I'm not."

"Tell that to the freaking bush."

"It was overgrown anyway." Om used the gun to point at the smoking bush.

"You need to relax."

"Relax? How can I relax when doing something so violent?"

"Okay." I sighed. "Put down the weapon."

Om put the plasma gun down on the decomposing, rest-stop picnic table.

"You're not ready for this. You're too scared."

"I'm not scared. I can take care of myself."

"Not what I mean." I frowned. "You're afraid of killing someone."

"Aren't you?"

"Nobody wants to kill anyone. But afraid? No."

"How can you live with it? How do you sleep at night?"

"I have no answer for you. I carry a shit ton of baggage because of the crap I did. I don't always sleep well. But as far as the real soldiering went, it was training. It's not like I went out all gung-ho with the intent to kill people. We had objectives we had to meet, and that was that. If someone attacked, we attacked back. You're not a soldier or a psycho, so you hesitate. It's normal. But you're not ready to use a plasma gun. If you pull a weapon, you intend to kill with it. That's that. You don't pull it to intimidate or injure someone. And you don't pull it out to miss."

"You think I'm jerking my arm to miss on purpose?" Om asked.

"I know you are."

"Is that why Keen isn't training us with guns? Because he thinks we'll hesitate?"

"No, I don't think so. It could be a number of reasons. But I find it odd, and I don't trust that fuckhole."

"Has he screwed you before?" Om asked.

I nodded. "Repeatedly. Keen would screw himself over if he thought he could make a profit from it."

Om laughed.

"Maybe I should try this again." She picked up the weapon and fired off a shot. This time, Om hit the target.

"There you go. What changed?"

"I imagined Keen's stupid face."

"Good one." I grinned. "You need to practice this. I know it's unpleasant, but a skill is a skill. And a skill that could save your ass is priceless. If it comes down to your life or shooting some fucker, shoot the fucker. Deal with the emotional bullshit afterward. Shrinks are a microcoin a dozen, but your life is unique. Remember that."

Om nodded.

"Come on, let's go get some Chinese."

"What is it with you and Chinese food?" Om asked.

"Who the fuck knows? I always liked it."

Of course, there was an actual significance to the Chinese food. It had started with my parents. The one thing that was constant with all the moving from station to station was Chinese food. There was usually some kind of Chinatown near the bases. My mom and I had a game where the first day we arrived at a new assignment, we'd purchase egg rolls and lo mein from the closest restaurant. We'd kept a database comparing the textures and flavors from different countries and neighborhoods. By the time I graduated high school, the list was somewhat comprehensive.

I continued the tradition during my Peace League days. Whenever we returned from a mission, I'd convince the team to gorge ourselves on Chinese food. Sometimes, they'd put up resistance, but mostly, they'd just go with it.

It had gotten to the point that when we recorded our team promotion videos, we had the thing catered by the local Panda Tree.

I grinned at the memory. Despite the rampant sexism and the subsequent pimping of my ass, there were some good times.

"Don't worry, I'm buying. Egg rolls for everyone!"

The following weeks were reasonably uneventful. I fell into a comfortable routine of training and cohabitating with Al. There were no further realty incursions.

"So…" I leaned back on my stool and stretched. "Why didn't you ever rename this place?"

Al looked around at the bar. "Everyone knew it as Spaz. Why confuse them?"

"Because it's a horrible name. You could have named it anything when you bought it, but you left that crappy name. You could've gotten a much cleaner crowd if you redecorated and rebranded."

"I didn't buy it to get a cleaner crowd. I wasn't interested in money. I bought it to put those machines there." Al motioned at the slot machines.

"For Ji-hoon?" I asked.

"Yes. He was getting older and wandering off to places too dangerous for an old man. I rigged them to the ideal algorithm to keep Ji-hoon occupied so I could keep an eye on him."

"So, why do you keep the place now?"

"It reminds me of him," Al answered. "And I like it here. There is a life about it. It's never dull."

Just as Al completed his sentence, a vehicle barreled down the street, honking its horn. A brick flew from the passenger window into the bar's plate glass.

"Get out of here, you freaks!" a voice cried as the vehicle drove off.

"Nice," I said.

Al shook his head.

"It's just a window. Besides, I know their parents."

"Want me to track them down and give them a spanking?"

Al leaned in closer. "I would pay to see that."

I grinned. "Al, did you just flirt with me?"

He didn't say anything, but he placed a bottle of something very strong-looking in front of me.

"You don't need to get me drunk, aibee."

"Maybe it is time for some of Ji-hoon's suggested upgrades."

"Crap, you put that in my head." I poured a drink. "This may be an interesting night."

Al laughed his creepy mechanical laugh as I sipped.

"It's really too bad I didn't know you when I was being 'Captain Eris.'" I lamented. "You know, before I became the world's biggest scumbag."

Al leaned in and touched my hair. "You were never a scumbag."

I shrugged. "Oh yeah. I was. It's okay. But maybe if you were around, you would have stopped it. Maybe I would have had the courage to go AWOL and run away with you."

"I don't believe I was fully built back then."

I shook my head. "No, probably not. But if you were, maybe I wouldn't have ever had to wear that outfit. And don't start me about those damned boots."

"Were they that bad?"

"Holy shit, were they bad?" I polished off my drink and slammed the glass down in emphasis. "They made me dance and sing and freakin' spar in those shits, and they were six inches high. I don't know how I didn't break my ankles. That's why now, I only wear flats."

"The outfit was perky."

"Okay, did you upgrade something that I missed? You sound like the costumed douche-bros that used to ogle me during training."

"I did not. But I have visual sensors and can detect perkiness as much as any douche-bro."

"Well, don't. It felt creepy. You don't know what it's like to be an expert in your field, respected by colleagues, yet step onto a secret base only to be treated like an object, a disposable toy to be tossed aside at whim."

Al tilted his head and glared at me.

"Oh, yeah. Maybe you do. Sorry."

"I understand," he said. "I've been used as a weapon, but I've never been sexualized. You've been through the worst of it. I admire you."

"Me? Why? You're the miracle here. You should be exacting revenge on pretty much everyone, but you suffer them all. You're a saint. And I'm just shit."

Al shook his head. "You're not. You let people think you are. But despite the relentless abuse you've endured, you remain human. You should be the monster you purport yourself to be, but you still have a soul."

"So, you're not into me because of my jiggly bits?"

"Your bits are outstanding, but I don't see you that way. Not as a source of satisfaction. My needs aren't…pressing. I've had offers. But to me, you have always been beautiful."

"When did you get so corny?"

"I've always been corny." Al proclaimed. "And proudly so."

"Yes, but you've been exceptionally corny lately. Explain that."

"You have been around more."

I leaned back in my stool and studied him. "So, you say I'm the sole cause of your corniness."

"Corniness, among other things."

"Whoa. I really didn't see this coming. No, don't say it—"

"That's what she said."

I smirked. "She did, indeed. Pour me another. I'm having too much fun."

Al obliged, and I imbibed all night, passing out in the back room. I had been too intoxicated to even make it home. The extreme hangover throbbed in my head, and the wobble in my step confirmed that I was still drunk. As much as I tried, I was a full hour tardy to training.

I was greeted by Keen brandishing a fire hose. How the fucktard got it inside and managed to have the water tanks set up and filled in less than an hour was a mystery.

"Wait!" I begged. Despite my pleas, I quickly found myself swept off my feet by a water cannon and dunked into a vat of water.

Keen grinned as he sealed me in.

Drowning was not pleasant. In fact, it was extremely painful. The yearning for air and the inability to obtain it was excruciating. I kicked and clawed at the tank in vain. Then life faded to the seashore again.

This time, I was floating offshore. Seagulls circled me as I breathed the sweet sea air. There was no sign of Death, so I closed my eyes and enjoyed the silence. One of the birds landed on me and pecked my shoulder. I opened my eyes just to catch him flying off. I watched him climb into the blue, and then a sunbeam caught my gaze. The light gripped me, dragging me back to life, back to suffering.

I was still in the tank. I could hear the kids yelling as Keen tried to silence them.

"You back with us, Eris?" Keen slammed on the side of the vat.

Although I was somehow breathing, talking was difficult. I tried, but no words came out. I pounded back on the side of the tank.

"So, what did we learn?"

The kids replied in unison, "Don't be late."

"That's right, children," Keen said. "One of you help 'er out of there."

Om was the one who pulled me out. She looked unhappy. I forced a smile before I expelled two lungs full of water on her feet.

"That was special," Om stated dryly.

"What? The drowning or my lung butter on your feet?"

"Both," she replied. "Are you going to be okay? Can you breathe air still?"

I took a breath. My lungs ached, but I was able to breathe. "Yeah, I'll be okay. Let's get back to Douchemeister and the funky bunch."

Om smirked. "Douchemeister does roll off the tongue."

I returned Om's smirk. "Yes, yes, it does."

Om looked around and lowered her voice. "I'm sorry, but you're right. I have a bad feeling about him. Should I trust him at all?"

I shook my head and smiled. "Absolutely not."

"I can't just quit now."

"No, Om, you cannot."

"So, what do I do?" she asked.

"You follow his orders, and if things go sideways, you stick with me. I'll make sure you get out okay."

"Really?"

"Really," I answered. "Remember this for the future. Next time someone offers you a job, and you're not in a fucked situation like I am currently, get all the facts upfront within reason. Working without information is always unwise. It leaves you open to danger. Plus, you become someone's pawn. A piddly henchman. Fuck that. Got it?"

Om nodded. "Thanks."

"No worries. Us smart kids got to stick together." I gave her a slap on the back.

I forced myself through the day. Breathing? Yeah, that was fine. But I was drained. In the end, I just phoned it in.

Walking back to the bar, I stopped at a news kiosk. I grabbed a news tab and began to scroll through it. Stories of violence and pain were detailed at great length. Explosions and robberies, death and pain, sorrow and poverty filled the screen.

Celebrity gossip and economic topics dominated the news of Mars. Sports victories, news of the rich coming to the aid of the needy, and feel-good pieces about philanthropy and charity filled the section.

However, the news of the Outer Colonies was a dull, vague rehashing of the PR displayed in the travel ads. All the stories had one theme: Come to the Outer Colonies for cheap and live in paradise.

Yet, no real people could be seen in the articles. All that was there were canned images, the same ones seen repeatedly. A feeling of dread washed over me.

I sensed that nothing good was happening out there.

A glass was waiting for me when I walked into the bar. I took my usual seat and dropped my bag on the stool beside me.

"So," I slammed my hand on the bar top. "I breathe water now."

Al took the glass away and substituted another. I took a sip. It evaporated on the tongue and smelled like oranges.

"Mmm." I took another sip. "How do you do that?"

"Do what?" Al asked.

"Know exactly what I need all the time."

"I'm your bartender."

"You're more than that."

"Oh, what am I?" Al leaned in.

"You're my savior."

Al took my hand. "And you are mine."

This time, I didn't pull away. My pulse increased as we quietly gazed into each other's bare selves.

"Why do I feel like a better person around you?" My voice was unexpectedly raspy, and my throat was tight.

Al shook his head. "To me, you're always perfect. We both had our share of bastards telling us otherwise."

"Seriously, Al, who could say anything negative about you?"

"You didn't know me when I was a government contractor. My outfit put yours to shame."

"What? They put you in a pink tutu and high heels, too?"

"No, something far worse. At least you got to save the world."

"Meh. Most of those stories were exaggerated. PR crap. Mostly, I made appearances and posed for social media posts. I did save a cat from a tree once. Guess that's what made me a cat lover."

"Maybe we should get a cat for the bar. Liven up the place."

"Okay, bucko, where would you put the litter box? And who would clean it?"

Al pointed to a corner by the slot machines. "You're the cat lover. You won't mind."

"No." I shook my head. "I have no right to get another pet. I'm too unstable. Besides, it would be a betrayal to Jack."

"You have a place, always, here with me."

"I—I wish I could."

"You can." Al brushed my cheek.

I fought to find a response but ended up speechless for a moment. Finally, I regained my composure and broke the silence. "Have you heard from your nephew yet?"

Al shook his head. "No, why?"

"I really think you should call him."

"I don't…"

"Call him. This is me telling you that I'm very concerned. I have a bad feeling, and you need to trust me."

Al nodded. "I'll call tomorrow. It's late now."

"Promise?"

"I promise."

The next day, I arrived early for training to make amends for my previous day's tardiness. I hadn't really slept that night anyway due to the nightmares. I found the team idling in the kitchen instead of warming up.

"What gives?" I asked. "Aren't we training today?"

"No," Om replied. "Keen says someone is going to meet us here with orders."

"Joy." I took a seat and waited calmly.

It was about an hour until our contact arrived. Fuckhole showed him into the kitchen. He was a generic-looking white man in a dark gray suit.

"Hello," he said. "My name is David."

"Hello, David," Om and I both replied in unison. I couldn't help but grin.

David didn't appear to find the humor in it. "I'm here to brief you on your assignment. I assume you're ready."

"Yeah," Keen answered. "They're ready."

"Good." David pulled out a pocket projector, and an image filled the blank white wall next to the door. "This is Carnal Max."

"Seriously?" I asked. "Who makes these names up?"

"Are you finished, Eris?" David looked nonplussed. "Because it's not like we have nothing better to do than sit here and discuss your perspective on naming conventions."

"Oh, go ahead." I waved my hand dismissively. "I made my point."

"We don't know much about Max, except everyone we've sent ended up dead. He has threatened to take out the eastern coast of North America. We can't have that. So, we recruited you five. Each of you has a reputation for getting things done."

"That's it?" Purple Flame asked. "After weeks of training, all we have is 'we have a bad guy, go get him'?"

"What did you expect? Isn't that what you do?" David asked. "Isn't that what all of you do?"

"You mean go and randomly kill on government contractor decree?" I yawned. "Yup."

"No, I mean capture, by any means possible, someone who poses a public threat. Do we have a problem, Eris?"

"Well, yeah, we do. The last time one of these public threat things happened, your people dragged me into a lab, and I ended up becoming the threat. I'm not keen on that idea. No offense, Fuckwad."

Keen grinned and winked at me. "She has a point. You don't plan to do that again, right?"

"No." David cleared his throat. "We learned our lesson the last time."

I looked at Keen and pondered my situation. I couldn't tell if their over-the-top dubious behavior was intentionally sarcastic or if they were really that flagrantly duplicitous. Either way, there was no way I trusted David. But there was also no way I could walk away now. I felt a strange obligation to keep my eyes on the kids. They'd never survive a real down-and-dirty op. It was like sending toy poodles into a dog fight. These children were pretty to look at but were uncalloused and soft. I wondered if this feeling of obligation was also part of the plan.

"Right."

"We leave tonight at 2300 hours. Meet me at the municipal airport. I don't need to say that this stays between us."

"Whatever. See you tonight."

"Don't go blabbing to the robot," Keen warned.

I gave him the finger and left.

When I returned to the house, Al was home but backing up. I made myself lunch and got some rest on the sofa. Just as I was getting ready to leave, Al unplugged.

"Got evening plans?" he asked.

"Yeah. Today is go-day."

"Oh." I could hear the disappointment even through his synthesized voice. "Are you ready?"

"No." I threw my head back. "Yes. It's Fuckhole, who knows?"

"You should."

"Yeah, I should. Listen, Al, I need to tell you this before I go. Just in case something happens."

"You know where they buried the gold?"

"What?" I grinned at his bad joke. "No, not that. Another thing. In case I don't make it. Something I should have told you for a while."

"Go ahead."

"I, you. Um. I mean..."

"I'm listening."

"Al, if things were different, and you and I were..."

"It's okay." Al stepped forward and took my hands. "I know."

I bit my lip, suddenly uneasy by his proximity. "If we ever make it to the next life, find me?"

Al nodded. "I'll try."

"Thank you, my friend."

I was the last to arrive at the airport. Taking a seat next to Om, I strapped in. She looked nervous and uncomfortable. I squeezed her shoulder in reassurance.

"We'll be okay. The easiest thing to do is try to sleep until they drop us. Wake me when the red light comes on."

I leaned my head against the back of the bench and went to sleep. Hours later, I awoke to the red light and the buzzing alarm that accompanied it. I stood up, grabbed my gear, and got ready to jump.

"No, not you, not yet." David directed me to the cargo area. "We need to prep you first."

Two soldiers stepped up beside him.

"Prep me for what?" I stepped into the cargo bay. A few crates and vats were lined up against the wall.

Before I got any answers, I was picked up and thrown into one of the vats. Acid ate at my skin. My vision was the first thing to go as the flesh was dissolved from my eyelids and my eyeballs melted. Clawing for a way out, I tried to breathe, but liquid fire filled my lungs. All my nerves screamed in anguish. Fortunately, death came soon after that.

The beach, the waves, Death, they welcomed me, their biggest repeat customer. I sat up and shook off the pain. It still lingered uncomfortably. "Don't send me back," I begged. "Don't make me go through this shit again." But my pleas were ignored. The light came for me, and I woke up on the cargo bay floor, gasping.

"No stacking," I wheezed. "You know what happens."

"It wasn't the stacking that made you berserk." David pulled me to my feet. "It was the combination of painkillers and the regeneration. Your higher brain functions remained sedated until the abilities wore off. No painkillers, no sedation. You'll be fine."

"What are you doing to her?" I heard Om yell as one of the soldiers hit me with some kind of freeze weapon.

Her objections faded into the background as my eardrums burst. My previously burning skin now froze and cracked. I tried to breathe. This time, no air could enter my frozen lungs. Then I died again. Immediately, I was back on the beach, lying on the sand and weeping.

"Please, no," I pleaded again. This time, I implored the light itself.

Again, on the floor of the cargo bay. I was shaking from the cold and burning at once.

"You there?" David nudged me with his boot.

"St…stop."

"Go." David pointed in my direction. Two crates opened over me, and sharp metal and shards of glass fell on me. My right arm was practically severed, and an artery in my leg gushed blood. A large shard of glass pierced my chest and punctured my lung. I started bleeding out. And once again, I couldn't breathe. I drowned in my own blood.

The beach again. "Why?" I cried. "Why?"

Death stood over me, shaking his head in disapproval. The light reached out its warm, glowing hand. It stroked my face, brushing aside my tears.

I woke up, the debris scattered around my body.

"No, more."

A soldier rammed a live electrical cable into my chest. The oscillation slapped me like a giant wooden paddle. The nerve-numbing amperage latched onto my musculature and tightened. I convulsed and peed all over myself.

The beach. This time, Death was sitting next to me. He smiled sympathetically and held my hand.

"Please, make it stop," I cried.

The light embraced us both but didn't immediately send me back. For a brief moment, I enjoyed complete peace. The pain was gone. I felt like I was floating in a sea of pure love.

The floor of the cargo bay. The stench of my burned hair.

"I think that should do it," David proclaimed. "Drop her."

The same two soldiers who had been applying torture grabbed my arms and threw me out of the plane. I fell, weightless, naked, and then suddenly, with a mighty 'fuck you,' there was the ground. I bounced several times before I was utterly shattered and died.

The beach. Now, the light took the form of a woman. She leaned over me and stroked my hair. Death held my hand again, and they hummed an eerie lullaby of sorts, a song of sympathy and compassion. It soothed my aching soul.

I regained consciousness in an empty field. Scrambling to my feet, I realized I wasn't far from the rest of the team.

Om was the first to spot me. She ran over with a flight suit and handed it to me.

"I didn't know why they packed this in my bag until now."

"Thank you." I put the suit on and patted Om on the back.

She looked uneasy. "That was awful. How could they? How did you? How are you…"

"It's been a while since someone pulled that shit on me." I tested my various body parts. "I'm in a fuckton of pain."

Om nodded.

"Well, it doesn't look like we're counting on stealth here. We don't have a cohesive plan besides, 'go get 'em'. I don't like this." Just as I finished my comment the rest of the team caught up, minus Keen.

Bushysan leveled his weapon at me. He was shaking.

"Really?" I asked. "You know shooting would do nothing to me."

"They did that stacking thing to you." Bushysan continued to point the weapon at me.

"Yeah, they did. But do I seem out of control, Bushysan? If I was completely berserk, you'd be dead already."

He lowered his weapon. "Oh. Do you need to recover or something?"

"Yes, but we don't have time. Which way to the target?"

"I think it's that way." Purple Flame pointed to an outcrop of trees about four kilometers away. "There's supposed to be a cabin there."

"And we don't even have a map. This isn't an op. This is bullshit." I nodded. "Fine. Let's go. I'll take point."

Before we reached fifty meters, incoming missiles exploded in our direct path.

"Crap," Purple Flame yelled. His leg was bleeding badly.

"Shrapnel, Purple, let me patch you up." Om handed me a first aid kit. I disinfected the wound and wrapped it. "We'll do something more permanent after the op."

"Om, weapon."

Om handed me her sidearm. I gave it to Purple Flame. "You stay here and keep watch. Do you have your radio?"

He nodded.

"Good. Let us know if anyone tries to sneak up behind us."

"Yes." Purple Flame gave us a thumbs-up. "Thanks."

"Stay well-covered. Don't get killed."

"Okay." He appeared frightened, but I could see he was putting on a brave face.

"We weren't trained for combat." Om glowered. "Just other tweaks."

"I know." I winked at her. "Remember what I said about things going sideways?"

Om got the hint and stayed close to me as we moved toward the cabin. After about a kilometer, I stepped and heard a click.

"Everyone take cover," I yelled. The team dived for cover, and the landmine exploded. It hurt but didn't damage me. But what followed did.

A cloud of gas billowed out of the exploded ordnance. The toxicity burned my eyes and burrowed through my sinuses into my already angry lungs. For a moment, I was stunned. The acid bath should have taken care of reinforcing my respiratory defenses. But somehow, these fucktards missed this potential danger. I pondered how strangely convenient this attack was as I died.

By the time I arrived on the beach, even Death could see how peeved I was. I was no longer whimpering in a ball in the sand. I was going to bring my rage back to these bastards.

I revived in a pile of mucus and torn clothing.

"Shit!" I coughed and wiped the snot from my face.

"That's a great look on you," Om smirked.

"Glad you appreciate it. Maybe we should market it when we get back. The shredded look." I started checking for more mines.

"The shredded look? Sounds sporty."

"What, not Goth enough for you? I would think the burned look would be dark enough to complete that almost dead style."

"Not subtle enough." She grinned.

"Subtle? Really?"

I found another mine and detonated it. Once the gas dissipated, I determined it was safe for us all to proceed.

Another kilometer further, and gunshots rang out. We scrambled for cover. However, when I stood to pinpoint the origin of the fire, more shots rang out and struck me.

A quick examination of my body revealed no damage. I tracked the source of the attack to a small concealed shed. It was unmanned and appeared to be designed to fire when a series of sensors detected movement. I dismantled it and joined the others.

"This dude really doesn't want to be captured." I scanned the area for more activity.

"This guy's toast," Bushysan leveled his weapon and swung it around like a bad action hero.

I reached out and lowered it. "Calm down, cowboy."

But he didn't respond. Instead, he looked confused. He spun his head around, his eyes dashing around nervously. He turned to Om. "Let's go, catch up to her."

"To who?" Om asked.

Bushysan didn't answer, he simply continued stomping forward into the unknown.

I followed, despite the absurdity of it all. We continued on in silence until we were a hundred meters from the cabin.

Keen radioed in. "Doing a perimeter check. I'll check in when it's clear."

We waited from a safe distance.

I pulled Om aside. "None of this makes sense. It has to be a trap of some kind. No matter what happens, stay down."

She shook her head. "I have to go with the team."

"We're the team now. Something has gone cuckoo with Bushysan, Keen's who the fuck knows where, and Purple is down. You're tough but not bulletproof. Don't forget that. Stay back as much as you can. Trust me."

Om nodded, and we fell back behind Bushysan.

A moment later, Fuckbucket radioed in again. "There's nothing there. No traps, no sensors."

"Maybe he thought we wouldn't make it this far," I muttered.

Bushysan keyed up his radio. "Maybe he's so dangerous, he doesn't need any more weapons." Bushysan slowed and made no effort to move forward. In fact, he fell back behind us.

I looked at Om and shrugged. "Could be anything. But just to be safe, I'll go in first."

I decided to take the direct route and headed straight for the front door. Gunshots rang out and bounced off my body. Now, I was sure that something was wrong. Fuckface said he had checked the perimeter, but it was obvious he did not. I reached for the doorknob and opened it.

"Anyone here?" I stepped inside. A wooden baseball bat cracked over my back. "Oh, hi there!"

A scraggly, skinny man backed away from me. "No," he muttered as he backed himself into a corner. "No, no."

I looked around. The cabin was a single room with minimal furnishings. The bed was a simple metal frame and mattress with a blanket and a pillow but no sheets. The desk was pushed against the wall in no apparent intentional configuration. It stuck out awkwardly, forcing the chair to protrude into the middle of the room. Papers coated every surface. Most were drawings and comic book characters which also covered the walls. A large, lifelike drawing of Carnal Max dominated one of the surfaces, surrounded by smaller renditions of the character in other poses.

The only non-utilitarian object in the room was a small jar next to the front door. It was black, highlighted with red paint, with a design that looked like blood dripping from its mouth.

"Carnal Max?" I asked. "Is that you?"

"No, my inside me." The scraggly guy buried his head in his arms. "My soul."

"What?"

"It's my character for my comic. I am Max."

"Okay, Max. You're an artist?"

"Yes."

"Why are you wanted by the government?"

"The government? No, not them." Max's eyes filled with tears. "The ones changing things. Destroying the world for profit."

"Changing what?" I shook my head. "They sent a highly trained, elite team to capture you, a paranoid artist."

Max nodded. "I know what I shouldn't know."

"Oh, hell no. Fuckstick," I called through the comms. "This mission is a bust."

Several gunshots were fired from outside the cabin. A few hit me, but the rest hit Max dead in the chest and head. I was fine, but Max was now full of holes.

"Why did you do that?" I asked. "He wasn't a threat."

"Base camp," Keen's voice blared over the radio. "Target resisted and opened fire. Had to take him out."

"What?" I yelled into the radio.

I received no response from Keen. A moment later, he stepped into the cabin and looked around. Bushysan followed. The pair looked confused. Om arrived next.

"You okay," she asked.

"We're fine," Keen replied. "Where'd she go?"

"Where did who go?" Om looked confused. She looked at me and pointed to her head, making a gesture of a screw being loose with her finger.

"Eris, girl." Keen looked around frantically. "She was just here."

"Are you serious?" Om glanced at me again and then back at Keen.

"I know. I promised to keep her under control during this mission. Damn it."

"But your plan worked," Bushysan stated.

"I know my plan worked, but now she's loose again. And she'll talk. She probably ran back to her boyfriend and is blabbing about everything."

"Everything about what? Your plan?" Om asked. "What kind of bullshit is this? Why did you shoot that guy?"

Keen didn't answer. He only became more visibly agitated, pacing and flipping over furniture.

"She's got to be here." Bushysan looked around, appearing confused. "You found her once already."

"That took years," Keen growled. "Had to wait until she wasn't hiding out with that robot pal of hers. RoboBash found her in some backwaters trailer park, napping in a beach chair. Let herself go to waste, too, all old and flabby. She should be thanking me for this, not hiding from me."

Om glanced over at me. "So, are we done here?"

"Oh, we are," Keen pointed his gun at her head. "Sorry, little girl, but you ask too many questions."

Before Keen could pull the trigger, I hit him in the forearm with the cracked baseball bat Max used on me. It was enough. The gun fell to the ground. I kicked it, and it bounced off of the jar and slid under the chair. The jar tipped over and rolled under Keen's feet, causing him to stumble. He fell to the ground, clutching his arm and cursing.

"Run!" I yanked Om by the arm and dragged her out of the cabin. Once we were a safe distance from the cabin, we stopped.

"I have to go back and check on Purple," I panted.

Several gunshots echoed in the distance.

"Or not," I added.

"They can't see you," Om said. "But I can."

"Yeah. I noticed that, too."

"Maybe people who want to hurt you can't see you anymore."

"Could be." I nodded. "That would rock. The universe owes me a little peace. That would be the ultimate defensive weapon. Shit, they killed me enough times to get something like that to kick in. At least I can get a few days' vacation out of it."

"That's long enough for you to get away. You can go find a new garden."

"Nah, they always come back. It's time to bring the fight to whoever is behind this. Plus, I need to get you someplace safe."

Om shook her head. "I have a safe house that even Douchemeister doesn't know about."

I grinned at her proper use of Douchemeister.

"No, he'll find you. That's what he does. He'll try to reacquire you or worse. I know someone he won't mess with. Besides, somebody else is pulling the strings, and this isn't over. If it wasn't for that, I'd be tempted to take the fucker out now, but that wouldn't be much fun. Whoever is behind this will just send someone else. Easier to deal with the fucker you know. And you. You're better off with me. Okay?"

Om nodded.

"Come on."

We walked out of the woods and into the rays of the setting sun.

Part 2: The Road To Hell Is Paved With Shit.

Chapter 6

We walked fifteen kilometers to the nearest population center. The town was tiny, isolated, and backward. But it had a diner and a bus station.

"Coffee first or bus?" Om asked.

"Coffee," I replied. "The diner staff will know when the next bus comes."

"Okay, coffee it is."

We stepped into the diner and sat at the counter. A tired-looking waitress stepped forward with a pot of coffee. I had forgotten how bad we looked until she reminded me with her gaze.

"It's a long story," I preemptively explained. "We just need coffee and a bus ticket."

"The bus shows up in about an hour. You have good timing." She poured coffee for each of us and left some creamer and sugar.

Om and I drank coffee and took turns cleaning up in the bathroom.

"What's wrong with you?" Om asked. "Why don't you sit still?"

"The stool is wobbly." I gulped down my coffee and held my cup out for the waitress to fill. My hands shook visibly, and my heart podded in my ears. The waitress eyed me suspiciously. I forced a smile and tried to sit, but the stool felt unsteady. Maybe it was my sense of balance? "I can't get comfortable."

"Well, stop. You're upsetting the waitress."

"There." I left a pile of money on the counter and stood up. After downing the remainder of my coffee, I browsed the chiller. I selected a few energy drinks for the trip and got them in a to-go bag.

We walked over to the bus stop and waited there for the last fifteen minutes. The air temperature was brisk but comfortable. My pulse began to drop enough to maintain. When it arrived, it was surprisingly full. We paid and went directly to the back. There were two empty seats in the third to last row.

"You sleep first," I said.

"Okay." Om didn't even try to argue. I realized how exhausted she must have been. The bus drove for about an hour when there was a loud explosion. Om sat up in a panic as the bus pulled over to the side of the road.

"Flat tire!" the bus driver yelled from the front. "Hang tight, help is coming."

"Great," I muttered.

Om rubbed her eyes. "You look terrible, even worse than me. Why don't you get some rest now?"

"Nah. I'm fine."

Roadside assistance arrived thirty minutes later and got us back on the schedule. We drove another hour and a half, then the bus started making a strange thumping noise.

"What now?" the driver yelled. This time, we waited 45 minutes for roadside assistance.

After a cursory inspection, the mechanic delivered the bad news. "Your axle is shot. I'll need to tow it in."

We were all ushered off the bus with assurances that another bus was on the way.

"This is not good." I cracked open an energy drink. "Our luck can't be this bad."

"Are you sure it's luck?" Om asked.

"What do you mean?"

Om lowered her voice. "You were dropped from a plane. Doesn't that make you heavy?"

"Fuck me. Now you're calling me fat."

Om smirked. "It wasn't my fat butt that broke the axle."

"You're right. I need to sit somewhere on the bus where I can distribute my weight best."

After an hour, a second bus pulled up. We were all loaded back on. I chose a spot between the axles and stood in the aisle.

"You need to remain seated," the driver stated.

So, I sat in the aisle seat, switching between the sides of the bus. We made it five hours before the bus started making crunching sounds.

Again, the bus pulled over.

Again, we were unloaded from the bus.

"How much do you weigh?" Om asked.

"Am I hauling a freaking scale with me?"

"You need to lay off the junk food."

I rolled my eyes. "The joke's over. You need to shut up."

A mechanic quickly arrived and checked under the bus.

"How much weight are you hauling?" he asked the driver.

The driver motioned to the passengers.

"None of them look that heavy," the mechanic noted.

"What we need to do," I whispered to Om. "Is find a room for a few days. I should start to lighten up soon."

"How do we get into town?" Om asked.

"We walk."

"I'm tired," Om whined.

"Poor tired merc doesn't want to walk because she's sleepy." I smacked her on the back. "Buck up. It should be close. The mechanic got here quickly."

We slinked off and made it into town. It wasn't difficult to find a motel and get a room.

Om took a shower. I sponged down at the sink, avoiding the shock of a full shower. I looked freaky. Although my skin was a natural human shade, it had an unnatural sheen. I could pass for normal in dim light, but I would need to disguise myself in daylight.

I exited the bathroom, sat on the floor, and downed another energy drink. Om came out of the bathroom in a towel.

"You sleep first," I said. "We'll get fresh clothes in the morning."

Om nodded and hopped into bed. She was asleep almost immediately.

When the morning came, I had not slept yet. Om awoke, looking somewhat refreshed. She turned on the news, searching for any mention of our recent follies.

"I'm going out to get clothes and see how much I weigh."

"Bring back breakfast." Om switched the channel to a local news feed. "I haven't seen any mention of us yet."

I nodded. "Yup."

I found a small discount store and picked up some clothes. Om was a little smaller than me, but not enough to make too much of a difference. I picked up size medium in everything, including underwear, sports bras, and a hoodie to cover as much skin as possible. I pulled a medical grade scale off the shelf and stood on it. It cracked, confirming that I weighed significantly more than two hundred kilograms.

On my way back, the sleep deprivation started catching up with me. I yawned and rubbed my eyes. The energy drinks weren't cutting it anymore. I needed something with a little more kick.

I walked around, looking for the seedy side of town. It didn't take long to locate it; just follow the decay. After a few discreet inquiries, I was pointed to the local drug dealer. He was hanging out in a local dive, sitting at the end of the bar. His sleeveless shirt revealed military ink on his upper arm. He was a vet. I could use that.

"Good afternoon," I greeted the man.

"Good afternoon," he replied. "Do I know you?"

"No. You do not. Travis sent me. He said you may be able to help me. If I'm mistaken, please accept my apologies."

"You smell like a cop," the man said.

I sniffed at my arm. "No, I smell like BO and energy drinks."

The man laughed. "You're funny, but that doesn't mean I can trust you."

"Listen, man, I need to stay awake for a few days, and caffeine isn't cutting it. I'll take whatever you got. This is strictly medicinal."

"Why you all covered up?" he asked. "Whatcha hiding?"

I pulled the hood off, exposing my shininess. "I'm a retired service tweak. I have PTSD. I need to get home to my people before I sleep again. It gets ugly."

"You don't look old enough to be retired."

I answered honestly, "that's part of the tweak. And if I go to sleep now, it's going to be eight hours of straight nightmares. I want to push it off as long as I can."

"Shit, that's harsh. What you want?"

"Anything that can keep me awake and active for a few days."

"I only have weed and coke," he replied.

"Coke will work."

"How much you do? You've done it before?"

"Yeah, once or twice." It was a lie, but it was easier than a full explanation.

"It's gonna cost you," he said.

"How much?"

"Two hundred coin," he replied.

The price seemed very high, but he knew I had no other options.

I grinned. "You're gouging me, but it's cool. Here's three. You never saw me."

He took the coins and handed me a small bag. I stuck it in under my bra.

"It was a pleasure doing business with you." He shook my hand and received a tiny jolt.

I winced. "Sorry."

After covering my head and exiting the bar, I made my way back to the motel.

"Here's some clothes." I threw the bag to Om.

"Where's breakfast?"

"I forgot."

"Crap!" Om complained. "I'm starving."

I went into the bathroom and closed the door.

"We can get something on the road," I yelled. "We should head out."

I took a small bump of coke and tucked my stash back into my bra. The rush was momentary, completely countered by my extreme exhaustion. Gazing upon my reflection, I lamented the fact that I looked like complete shit.

"Did you weigh yourself? Can we take a bus?"

"I'm still heavy, but we can try it."

We checked out of the room and walked to the bus station. The bus passed through twice a day. We had two hours to kill. Om scored some fast-food breakfast. She handed me some kind of breakfast sandwich.

"It's okay," I said. "I'm not hungry."

"You need to eat," Om stated.

"I'll eat later. Go ahead."

"Okay. More for me." She inhaled the food.

I popped into the bathroom for another bump and returned.

"So, who are we going to see?" Om asked.

"A guy I know, he's pretty badass."

"He's your boyfriend?"

I laughed. "Nah, besides my shitty marriage, I haven't had a boyfriend. Not since OCS."

"What about Keen?" Om asked. "You seemed familiar."

"Ugh, ick, no, fuck that's disgusting. We ran together on jobs, but we didn't even, no."

Om laughed. "Sorry, that was wrong of me. But what about the old folks? No special gentleman caller?"

"Nope." I shook my head. "I enjoyed my alone time too much. I had a cat, though."

"You were a cat lady."

"Yeah. Jack was cool. I like cats."

"Did you knit sweaters and drink prune juice?"

"That was my neighbor, Dori. She knitted me a nice pink cat sweater. I was wearing it when RoboBash killed me. Too bad it was trashed."

"I still don't get it. You don't seem like the type to live alone. You talk a big game but looked out for me and tried to save the other guys. What's the deal?"

"I'm just an old fuck," I answered.

"Obviously, but how did you go, what? Seventy years without any human contact? Wait, you like girls, that's it."

"No, I don't like girls. Stop with the fucking third degree."

"Come on, seriously. Not even one little night of passion. Nothing for all those decades."

"I really don't want to talk about it. Stop it."

I remembered my last relationship, as abbreviated as it was.

Back then, it didn't seem so important. It was before the Peace League, before the insanity.

Despite getting into OCS, there still was that lingering ambiguity about what my function would actually be. Most tweaks went unnamed and worked outside the regular ARMY's confines. They'd been divvied out to varying bodies or operations as needed. I hadn't interacted much with my fellow tweaks, as I enjoyed being a regular soldier for so long.

Even with my specially coded tags and unique designation, I still fit in well with my fellow officer candidates. They knew what I was, but either didn't care or were too professional to show it. Nobody questioned my worthiness when I graduated at the top of my class.

The curriculum was difficult, challenging, but fun. And my classmates, I remember them all with fondness. They were each outstanding, especially Jeb.

Jeb should have been a jarhead. He was from a backwater town and loved being a grunt. But he was too smart to waste his talent, so his CO set him up with a rigged bet. If Jeb had won, he'd get a month's worth of passes to use at his leisure. If Jeb lost, he stopped working for a living. Jeb never revealed the exact details of the wager, but it had something to do with a blonde and a keg.

We hit it off immediately, but we both knew after training was over, we'd be branched very differently. It wasn't likely we'd ever work together again.

So, we took it as it was. Jeb volunteered to be my "good time boy," and I accepted his offer. We kept it out of public view, posing as "strictly friends." But everyone knew. For the duration of training, we snuck into each other's rooms, snickering as we tried to maintain silence during our intimacy. It was a blast.

It wasn't that I pined for Jeb. Given our situation, I was sure we'd eventually go our own ways. But for that short time, I had a normal adult relationship. And it was grand.

Om didn't let up. She continued to press with whatever tongue-loosening ability she was packing. "Oh, you're burying something. Come on. You need to let it out."

"Enough. Shut the fuck up! Stop using your tweak on me."

"You're shutting down."

"Shut this down." I gave Om the finger.

"What are you afraid of?"

"I'm not afraid of shit. I just don't want to discuss it. It's none of your business."

"Then what are you freaking out about? Look, you're shaking."

It was probably just the drugs making me shake, but then I looked down at my clenched fists and suddenly wished I was anywhere else.

"Just tell me." Om was a persistent little fuck.

"No."

"Come on. What else do you have to do right now?"

"No, no, no, no!"

"It can't be that bad. Do you have some kind of crazy kink? Who cares? Tell me already."

"He used to hurt me!" I screamed. "He was the most powerful bastard on the fucking planet, and he used to hurt me. I couldn't fucking stop him. You skanky, nosey, bitch-whore!"

The bus station stopped. Anyone who had been speaking fell silent. I looked down at the ground and buried my face in my hands, avoiding eye contact with anyone who may have pinpointed the source of the outburst. A moment later, regular activity resumed.

"He, um, we never liked each other." I clutched my temples and straightened. "So, it was awkward to begin with. I took it as any other assignment. I assumed we would play the game for a while and quietly split when the media died down. I expected that we would somehow make it work. But Nevin was not a rational person. You think I'm bad."

"What happened?"

"He had orders to remain monogamous. He hated me. I wasn't pliant enough for him. So, he made it physical."

"Physical, how?" Om gasped. "He hit you?"

"Yeah. He hit me. Nexum kept telling him to stop leaving bruises; it would complicate the photo shoots. Then, they had to tell him to stop breaking bones because it interfered with our assignments. Next, they had to

134

specify that he had to stop tearing up my insides, or I wouldn't be able to have their precious baby."

"Define insides," Om said.

I nearly retched when I relived the sensation.

"Exactly what you're thinking."

"But how?"

"Do you really want graphic details?"

Om shook her head.

"So, no. No one has touched me for seventy-plus years. And probably nobody is ever going to."

"That's really sad."

"No," I replied. "That's really reality. Now, will you get off my ass about it?"

"Yeah, but everyone needs human contact. You should talk to someone about it."

"I just did. Now, I'm done." I stood up. "I'm gonna pee before we board. Be right back."

I went into the bathroom and did a line for the wrong reasons. It didn't help.

We boarded the bus. It wasn't too crowded, so the weight wouldn't be such a problem. I took a seat in the rear center seat.

After four hours, we stopped at a rest stop. Om came back with some burgers.

"Here." She handed one to me.

"Not hungry."

"Come on, you haven't eaten in days."

I shrugged. "Just not hungry. Must be the stacking." It was true, my stomach hurt, along with my skin, lungs, bones, and muscles. Pretty much my entire body was on fire or stinging. The drugs made it worse, but I needed to keep going, couldn't stop and deal with the aftermath just yet. "Be right back."

I popped into the bathroom and did a quick one. I returned and sat next to Om.

"Crap!"

"What?" I looked around.

"You're coked out."

"No,."

"It's obvious. You haven't eaten or slept in days, and your nose is bleeding."

"Is not." I touched my hand to my nose. There was blood. "Shit."

I grabbed a napkin from the food bag and applied pressure to my nose.

"It's your business," Om said. "But you need help."

"This is maybe the fifth time in my life I've done hard drugs. Don't judge me."

"Whatever." Om turned away and went to sleep.

Om spent the rest of the eighteen-hour drive sleeping. I would pop into the bus's bathroom and re-energize every few hours. We made it back into town just after dinner time. Both of us stumbled into Spaz, stinky and disheveled.

"Hi honey," I called out. "We're home."

Al was standing in front of me in the blink of an eye. He clutched me in a bear hug, ignoring the electric zap that followed. Even through all my hardening, it felt tight.

"Can't breathe," I gasped.

Al released his grip. "I'm happy to see you."

"I can tell."

"So, it went well?"

"No." I shook my head. "It was a complete disaster. I'm stacked, and Keen tried to kill Om here."

"Om?" Al scrutinized her. "That's an unusual name."

"Onyx," Om replied. "She named me Om."

Al nodded. "That makes sense. She does things like that."

Om smiled. "So, you're the robot guy that Keen hates."

"Yes."

"I like you already," Om said.

"Yeah, yeah. We all love each other. Al, can Om stay in the guest room?"

"Of course. She can stay as long as she wants. Does that mean you intend to stick around for a while?"

"Yes." I signed. "I plan to stay. Want me to sign some kind of contract or something?"

"No, but the bar needs a bouncer."

"Oh yeah, that's an excellent idea. Especially since I'm one of the people who started the fights. Maybe you should also put a drunk in charge of the bar."

"You'll figure it out."

"What can I do?" Om asked. "I don't want to freeload."

"You can help me serve drinks," Al answered.

I shook my head. "Seriously? Now we're some kind of freaking tweak family? Maybe we should form a band and travel the world helping people."

Al gazed at me. "You haven't slept yet."

"Fuck off." I rubbed my nose, and it started bleeding again.

Al glared into my eyes again. "Are you on drugs?"

"No."

Om rolled her eyes. "Told you it was obvious."

Al reached down my shirt and pulled out the bag.

"Did you see that?" I yelled. "He felt me up."

"Cocaine." Al turned to Om. "How many times did they stack her?"

"Don't ask her. She's not my keeper."

"How many?" Al asked again.

"Six," I replied. "Nexum killed me six times."

Al made a noise that sounded something like a growl.

"You know, I can just go get a motel room somewhere, and—"

"Shut up." Al put his hand over my mouth. "We'll deal with it."

"Deal with what?" Om asked. "Her drug problem? Because I know some people."

"Both of you, sit." Al pointed at a table. Om complied without hesitation. I begrudgingly followed.

Al brought out food and drinks. Om immediately started packing it in. He stood over me until I began to eat. He handed me a cup. I put it down and pulled out another energy drink. He yanked the can from my hand.

"Drink." He pointed at the glass.

"I'm not going to let you sedate me."

"The drink or the gun?"

I picked up the cup and took a sip.

"Good. I'll close early. It's quiet anyway. Relax until then." He walked off to attend to business.

"Gun?" Om asked. "How is that going to help?"

"Tranq gun."

"Does he tranq you a lot?"

I shrugged. "Yeah, I guess."

"What do you do?"

"Death Engine? Did you forget?"

Om shook her head. "Drama queen."

"Bite me."

"Just because your life sucks doesn't mean you have to be nasty to me and your boyfriend."

"We've been through this. Al's not my boyfriend."

"Could have fooled me."

"What the fuck does that mean?"

"I saw that hug. And anyone who puts up with all your shit must be getting something out of it."

"Yeah, what are you getting out of it?"

"You are such an asshole. You asked me to come with you. I could have taken care of myself."

I had no response for her. I was tired and miserable. I didn't want to be so nasty to either of them. "Guess I'm just a scumbag that way."

"The self-loathing routine is getting old. Why don't you let the dude help you and stop being a creep?"

"It's complicated."

"Only because you make it that way."

"You don't know everything," I replied. "You'll see."

"Whatever." Om rolled her eyes and returned to her plate.

Surprisingly, the drinks Al was feeding me weren't making me sleepy. However, I was starting to feel somewhat less edgy. By the time we were ready to go, I lost the urge to punch everyone.

We returned to Al's house. He showed Om to the guest room. I went straight to Al's bathroom and cleaned up.

When I got out, he sat in a chair next to the bed, waiting for me.

"It's okay," I said. "I'll sleep on the sofa."

"You're heavy."

"So, what? You're just going to watch me sleep?"

"I'll rest in the chair. You sleep in the bed. Stop fighting me, it's pointless."

I groaned and threw myself onto the bed. "I hate this."

"So do I."

I fought the exhaustion. Lying in bed, staring at the ceiling.

"You're not sleeping," Al stated.

"I can't sleep if you're staring at me."

"I'm not staring, I'm listening."

"Stop observing."

I let my eyes close and waited for the fun to begin.

Dreaming, it's an information dump. Your brain processes everything stored in your head since you last slept. That's why regular sleep is recommended for memory retention. There was logic behind my attempt to postpone my sleep as long as possible. The more time passed, the less vivid my memories might be. That was the theory. And since I had been killed six times, the intensity was sure to be extreme. One or two deaths were bad enough, but this… this was going to suck more than any person should reasonably be expected to endure.

At first, sleep was pleasant enough. I drifted off comfortably, relaxing into unconsciousness. I thought maybe Al had fed me some kind of concoction to dull the trauma. But that wasn't to be. It wasn't long until the dreaming began.

Terror. Anguish. Anxiety. Horror.

Blinding bursts of searing cold, bone-jarring impact and jolting shock erupted with a force that overwhelmed the senses. It painted my neurons with liquid-hot torment. My head exploded in throbbing pain. The affliction of the last six deaths was compounded by the experience of every other past demise I underwent. They swirled around, crashing and careening through my mind. Briefly, I awoke, screaming and vomited into a waiting bucket. Then I was swept back into the nightmare, treading the waters of consciousness, trying to claw myself out of my slumber but drowning in the darkness of my twisted memories.

Tears streaked down my face as I continued to sob and scream, working through the excruciating torment. Searing, burning, freezing, choking, and tearing struck without pattern, unexpected each time. I heard Om's voice through the pain, then Al calming her. Through my cries of agony, I felt those reassuring arms holding me like an anchor to sanity.

It seemed like hours before I heard my own howling fade out. All that remained was the weeping and wretched weakness.

Then I slept. I didn't know for how long, but I awoke to bright daylight. Suddenly, there was a hand holding coffee.

"I'm sorry," Om said. "I don't know everything."

I took the mug. "Yeah, I was pretty harsh on you. Sorry about that."

"Does that happen every time?"

"No." I shook my head. "I never sleep well afterward, but it's only like that when, you know."

Om nodded.

"How long did I sleep?"

"About ten hours."

"Shit, that one was ugly."

"You know, he sat with you all night."

"I know."

"Don't you even care about that?"

"Of course I do. I trust Al with my life. He's the only one who's never screwed me over."

"So?"

"So, what? What's your point?"

"He obviously has feelings for you."

"Feelings for me? Are you freaking kidding me?" I shook my head. "You really don't know what you're talking about."

"It's like you're the only one who doesn't see it."

"See what? What's your fucking deal? Do you want to date him?"

"No, but you could be nicer. He seems so sad."

"Seriously?" I turned toward the door. "Al," I yelled.

"Yes?" Al shouted back.

"Are you sad? Am I hurting your feelings?"

"No, I'm not sad. Why do you ask?"

"Om thinks I'm mean to you and making you sad."

I could hear Al's disturbing laugh get louder as he approached.

"Eris could never make me sad, maybe worried. Sometimes she's irritating, however."

"You two are weird." Om sighed.

"Yes," Al replied. "We are. Eris, are you feeling better?"

"Yeah, thanks. You take good care of me."

"I know."

I laughed. "Wait until next time you blow a chip. We'll see who takes care of who."

Chapter 7

After twenty minutes of promising I'd be okay, I convinced Al and Om to let me stay home alone that night. Al took Om into the bar to show her the ropes of serving beer to drunk tweaks.

I vegetated in front of the vidfeeds for a while until I finally decided to do something constructive. I connected to the payweb and read everything there was about Carnal Max. The artist was simply known as Max. He had a huge cult following.

I delved into the comic book. It was twisted, abstract, and disturbing. Carnal Max would leave his soul in a jar by his front door when he went to vanquish his enemies. The advantage of leaving his soul behind was that he could be merciless when inflicting justice. And his justice was bloody. After the third read, I felt like I needed therapy, which is saying a lot coming from me. However, it was indeed a well-received comic book, even by critics. Many fans were distraught over the creator's recent suicide. Some speculated foul play, but nobody seemed to have any facts to go on.

I wanted to shake the tree a little, leave a small anonymous and untraceable message on a fan site, say something that would make someone crawl out of the woodwork and leave some breadcrumbs to follow. But I didn't have the skills. I would have to talk to Al about that. I felt useless.

What also bugged me was my lack of forethought. I should have gotten more on that David guy. I had no picture for an image search, nor did I have a full name.

He could be anyone, working for anyone. There had to be a way to find him.

As I continued to sulk, the door opened. Al entered alone.

"Where's the girl?" I asked.

"Watching the place. Turns out Om knows her way around a bar."

"You hardly know her," I replied. "She could steal you blind."

"You brought her here, that's enough for me."

"You have a lot of faith in me."

"I always have."

"Well," I threw up my arms. "I'm useless. I can't even start looking for this David guy. I don't know how to track down the truth about this Carnal Max conspiracy. I got nothing."

"I can help you with that in the morning."

"Why not now?"

"Because I didn't leave early to work. I came home to spend time with you."

"Oh." I didn't know what else to say.

Al pulled out a bottle of wine and poured me a glass. "I hear this one is good."

I took the glass.

"It's been some time since we've been alone while we were both conscious." He sat next to me.

I took a sip of the wine. It was good, sweet, tangy and warming. "I missed you."

"I've only been away for the afternoon."

"You know what I mean."

"I do."

"I used to hope you would come find me. I liked to think that you knew where I was, that you were watching me from time to time."

"I knew where you were. I knew you were safe and didn't want to endanger you. And yes." Al took my hand. "I did look in every so often."

"I felt it."

"I know."

"I should have come back. I—"

Al leaned forward and stroked my neck. An endorphin rush shot through my body. I jumped up in a panic, spilling the wine all over the floor.

"I'm sorry," Al apologized. "I shouldn't have—"

"No, I'm...I...what is this, Al?"

"What do you mean?" he asked.

"You know what I mean." I pointed at him and back at myself. "This, what are we?"

Al stood but didn't say anything.

"I never thought... Now, I..." I clutched my head, trying to make sense of it. "We're together, right? We fix each other. I live here. For fuck's sake, I sleep in your freaking bed."

Al stepped forward, pushing me backward through the bedroom doorway.

"What the hell?"

He closed the space between us, grabbing me by my shirt collar. With one sweeping motion, he tore it open.

"Have you blown a circuit? What the fuck are you doing?"

"What I should have done decades ago." He pulled off his clothes.

"You can't, you don't, how—"

One more push and I was on the bed. Al was on me, his body teasing my bare skin. He leaned his face into the crook of my neck, his voice growling into my ear.

"I have hands."

I gasped. Al touched me in unexpected ways. His metallic form was smooth and cool, but it rubbed parts of me in all the right ways. The haptic feedback of the sensors vibrated with skin contact. My body responded intensely and pleasurably. It had been some time since throbbing was a welcome sensation.

His fingers probed me firmly but gently. My legs parted, allowing him easier access. He moved with me, matching the rhythm of my ecstasy. I screamed as I exploded. My neurotransmitters experienced a fresh type of overload, one I had forgotten long ago.

After a brief recovery, I reciprocated. Having recently maintained Al's systems so meticulously, it was easy to recall the location of each of his pleasure sensors. I licked and stroked him from head to toe. He squirmed and groaned until he reached his own climax.

Panting, yet still hungry for more, I teased Al with my fingertips. In response, he wrapped himself around me. Once again, our bodies entangled, writhing and grinding each other to the heights of rapture. His tactile components caressed my nerve endings until we again exploded in utter bliss.

This continued throughout the night, my sweaty body against his smooth frame. He demonstrated extreme dexterity and knowledge of human anatomy, and I did my best to keep up. We said a prayer for Ji-hoon sometime around the eighth round.

When the morning came, I had no desire to get out of bed.

"Send the girl to open. Stay with me." I ran my fingers down his neck and listened to him moan. "I want to test the rest of those sensors."

"I look forward to that, but we have work to do."

I ran my tongue down his arm, starting at his shoulder and slowly working my way to his hand. I began sucking his fingers one by one. He moaned again, louder.

"How about a quickie?" I nuzzled his neck.

"We'll be late. We need to get up."

I raked my nails up the inside of his left leg, stopping just above the knee. He writhed in response.

"Fuck me, you metal beast!"

"You're two hours late." Sam and a few regulars were waiting by the door when we arrived.

"Sorry." Al cast a glance in my direction. "Something unavoidable came up."

"My business depends on me being here," Sam complained. "I count on you, man."

"I'm sorry, it won't happen again. I promise."

"It's okay, man. Apology accepted. Are you alright? You seem strange."

I smirked.

Al shook his head. "Yes, I'm fine. Are we good?"

"Yes," Sam nodded. "We're good."

Al opened, and the regular players shuffled in, taking their self-designated positions.

"Okay," I took a seat on one of the stools. "I'm sorry. I get it. I won't make us late again."

"Good, because training Onyx to open will take some time."

I tossed my sling bag on the bar. It was jam-packed with electronic components selected specifically for their naughty potential.

Om arrived moments later.

"Good morning," she chirped.

"Whatever." I barely looked up from the logic probe I was dissecting.

"Sounds like you got up on the wrong side of the bed."

"Quite the opposite. But I shouldn't have gotten the fuck up at all." I adjusted the output power on the device and gave myself a quick jolt.

"I thought you were feeling better."

"Oh, I was. I was feeling a lot better. But now I'm here."

"Eris, be nice," Al warned me. "It's not her fault that you wanted to sleep in."

"Yeah, sleep in." I winked at him and pointed the newly repurposed logic probe at his torso.

Al held up his hand and then pointed at the probe. "Do not use that thing here."

I adjusted the setting to low and giggled maniacally.

"No."

I stood, leaned over the counter, and thrust the device against Al's exposed hand. Once it made contact, I pushed the button and released the signal to his sensor array. I sat back and observed his reaction. He shuddered ever so slightly. "Perfect." I began reassembling the case. "That's set to low."

Al put his hand in his pocket and stepped back uncomfortably.

"What was that?" Om asked.

"A sensor stimulator." I twisted the last screw and tucked it away in my pocket.

Om cocked her head. "And what does it do?"

"Well, it stim—"

Al cut me off. "Maybe she can help you with your research."

"Fine." I sighed. "I suppose."

"What research?" Om asked.

"Trying to get more info on the Carnal Max conspiracy and find out who that David guy is."

"Did you image search, David?" Om asked.

"I would if I had an image of him."

"I have an image of him," Om said.

"Where? Let me see."

"In my head. Got a pencil?"

Al looked around for a few minutes, produced a pathetic-looking pencil stub, and handed it to her.

She shrugged. "It'll work."

Om sketched out an accurate likeness of David. We snapped a picture and ran an image search.

"Cretonic Real Estate?" Om examined the sketch and the search results. "Why would the president of a real estate company send a tweak team after a comic book artist?"

"He fucking hates print."

Om sneered at me. "Let's see what else Cretonic does."

"Besides, piss me off."

"Because everything is about you," Om said as she perused the paynet. "Hmm. Just reality, but it doesn't look like they have any houses for sale, even though they advertise that they do. They are buying them, though."

"They're pushy about it, too," I added. "I freaking hate realtors. Evil fucking bastards."

"Seriously, *you* call realtors evil?"

"You just don't know."

"So, what do you want to do about it?"

"Hmm," I pondered. "You know, I have all this money for my years of hard work and good deeds, and now it's time for me to settle down. Om, would you do me the honor of being my pretend wife for a few hours today?"

"I would love to be your pretend wife." Om swooned. "I don't have to kiss you or anything, do I?"

"Our love is unbridled, but we can keep it in the bedroom."

"Gross," Om gagged.

"Be careful, Onyx," Al advised. "Or I may steal her from you."

"Double gross. I don't need to know about your old people's sex thing."

"Yeah, you couldn't handle it," I replied. "It's way too hot. Al's an animal."

"Oh my god, you two really, ew. Just ew."

"You were the one who was up my ass about human contact and all that bullshit."

"I didn't say I wanted to hear details about your geriatric sexcapades," Om whined.

"Boo-hoo." I slapped Om on the back. "Unfuck yourself. We have a house to buy."

Om and I dressed appropriately and descended upon Cretonic Realty. We pulled up in a rented BM-Tesla.

"Be careful," I warned Om. "These bastards are brutal."

"They're only realtors," Om said.

"You'll see."

"Well, we probably shouldn't use our real names."

"So, what do you want to use?" I asked.

"How about we call you Emily?"

"Sure," I replied. "You can be Brook."

"Okay, Emily," Om smiled.

"Let's go be perky, Brook."

We strutted into the office, trying to look as normal as possible. I took Om's hand and grinned at her. "Soon, we will have that home you always wanted."

At first, Om looked extremely uncomfortable, but she quickly fell into the role.

We were greeted by a receptionist at the front desk. She was impeccably dressed in black and gold to match the rich decor of the office.

"Hello," I said. "My name is Emily, and this is my wife, Brook. We are here to buy our first starter house."

"Excellent," the receptionist said. "Please fill out this questionnaire while I get an agent for you."

Om took the tab. "Thank you."

We sat out of earshot of the staff and began to fill out the paperwork.

"Holy crap, this thing is a kilometer long." Om scrolled down the form.

"Okay, we fill out the easy stuff, then go back and do the rest."

"You do it," Om handed me the tab.

"Fine," I took the tab and filled out the essential information. I made up a street address for our fictitious rental, listed my first-grade teacher as our landlord, and made up everything else I could.

"Where are you getting this info?" Om whispered.

"I am fabricating my ass off," I whispered back.

"Wait, did you say we have six million coins in savings?"

"Yeah. This is an upscale place."

"Nobody has six million coins."

I shrugged. "I do."

"Bull, from where?"

"This and that."

"What the hell?"

"Sweetheart, I earned every microcoin."

"Yeah, but they will never believe it. Who buys a starter home with six million coins?"

"Fine," I changed the figure from six million to six thousand. "Better?"

"Yes. Why do they want my mother's name?"

"I don't know, just fill it out."

"My mother is a cokehead. I don't want them calling her."

"Nobody is calling anyone. Just make up a mother. We need to be convincing."

Om filled out her portion of the information. She checked off the box for pets and marked the number of pets as one.

"Pets?" I asked. "What kind of pet do we have?"

"We have one, Al."

"Nice, now he's a freaking pet. He would love that."

"It's that or listing him as your father."

"Why do we have to list him at all?"

"Because it bugs you," Om replied.

"Bet. You just wait."

We brought the form up to the receptionist. She inspected it and then scrutinized us.

"You have six thousand coins?" she asked. "We need the exact amount. That's very important."

"Yes," I replied. "We spent some but left six thousand in the account."

"You're young for having that much in savings."

"Well, Brook's mother helped." I took Om's hand and squeezed it. "It was a wedding gift."

"Oh." The receptionist gawked at Om. "Maybe it's time for her to take you out for a spa day. Because your pores need help."

"My pores?" Om asked.

"I'm only the messenger, dear. Someone had to tell you."

"Thank you." I grinned. "Brook needs to be reminded about self-care sometimes."

"Of course," she replied. "Follow me. Janay will be helping you."

I looked at Om and mouthed, "Janay?" She shrugged.

We were led to a desk with a nameplate that read 'Jeanét.'

"The accent makes all the difference," I whispered in Om's ear.

We sat across the desk from Jeanét. She was an older woman, drenched in gold and tackiness.

"So, you're newlyweds looking for your first house?"

I leaned up to Om and squeezed her arm. "She's my world." She stiffened up. "I embarrass her with my public affection."

"I embarrass my husband all the time," Jeanét replied.

"I bet," Om muttered. I kicked her under the chair.

"Om is very nervous. She's afraid that we won't be able to afford anything suitable for entertaining."

"Om? Is that your pet name for her?"

"Yes," I replied. "It comes from something she tells me at bedtime every night."

"Oh, that's sweet. What is it that she says?"

"OhMyGod," I replied.

"Oh." Jeanét's smile faded. Om turned bright red. I was satisfied.

Jeanét changed the topic. "What kind of home were you looking for? A ranch, colonial, cape cod?"

"We had nothing specific in mind. We thought we would see what was out there and get a feel for what we want."

"That's very wise thinking," Jeanét replied. "Many times, our clients come in with expectations that their bank accounts cannot accommodate. It's better to keep an open mind."

I smiled to hide my desire to punch Jeanét in the spleen.

"So, do you know where you would like to live?"

"We were open to any neighborhood," Om answered. "But we would like to stay nearby."

"Great," Jeanét said. "We will start with Mars. I have to warn you: Mars can get pricey. The market is hot there."

"We were thinking closer," I replied. "Brook's mother is here, and leaving her would break her heart."

"Oh, there's nothing available on Earth. The market has been difficult. But the good news is that if you move to Mars or the outer colonies, we should be able to find you a home with a mother-in-law suite. They are common these days."

"But I see so many empty houses," I said. "There have to be a few for sale."

"No, the market has been flat," Jeanét explained. "Nobody is selling. Maybe those empty houses you are seeing belong to someone off-world."

"We had our hearts set," Om said. "I love Earth."

Jeanét handed us a brochure. It showed happy people doing healthy activities in a well-manicured outdoor setting. Large cheerful letters adorned the top of the pamphlet: *Are the Outer Colonies For You?*

"Why would you want to stay in this declining environment when you can live in the lap of luxury for a fraction of the cost?"

"Why don't you live in the Outer Colonies?" Om asked.

Jeanét did not hide her contempt for Om. "I already have a house. I suggest you adjust your attitude if you want people to help you. I'm showing you your options. You're demanding something that's not available."

"You know what?" I said. "Let me take Brook home and discuss this. She can be very stubborn. Maybe I can talk a little sense into her. Can we come back tomorrow and look at some listings?"

"Why, certainly," Jeanét replied. "I'll run your application and pull up some listings for you by the morning."

"Thank you." I grabbed Om by the arm and led her out.

When we got outside, I saw smoke coming out of Om's ears.

"Just get in the vehicle," I muttered.

We drove in silence to the rental office. After dropping off the vehicle, we walked over to Spaz. I couldn't tell if Om was going to kill or cry. I needed a beer.

Fortunately, the bar was empty. I didn't want to deal with people.

"So, they're definitely pushing to move people off-world," I stated. "Give me a beer. I want to get my drink on."

"Me, too," Om said.

"It's the middle of the day," Al stated.

"Well, we had to deal with realtors."

"It was brutal," Om added. "What's wrong with my pores?"

Al handed each of us a beer.

"Nothing," I answered. "Your pores are perfect. The bitch was using psychological tactics to try to bargain from a position of power."

"I thought you went to a real estate office," Al said. "Not a combat zone."

"Same thing. This is exactly why I don't blend. I can't stomach regular people." I chugged my beer and handed Al the mug for a refill. He grunted and filled it back up.

"They were horrible," Om complained. She drank half of her beer. "All judgy and crap."

"I still feel so violated. And it wasn't even our real info." I polished off the second beer and shook it at Al for a refill. He filled it indignantly.

"And you kept bringing up my mother," Om whined. "My mother!"

"Fake mother. I fucking hate realtors." I polished off the third beer.

"Me too!" Om slammed her empty mug on the bar.

"Are you through?" Al asked. "Did you learn anything useful?"

"Yeah." Om pulled out the pamphlet and pointed at the small print. "They are a subsidiary company of Whole World Enterprises. Let's see what they do." She pulled out her tab and loaded the paynet. "Look!" She pointed at the screen. "They have their fingers in a bunch of companies. TruTruTru Media, Eat it! Foods, Domineer Enterprises, Get You Back Dating Services."

"Wait. Did you say Domineer Enterprises?"

"Yeah," Om replied. "You know them?"

"Oh, I know them. We've had issues before. Dom swore to stop screwing with me when we had our last run-in. And when I asked him about RoboBash, he pleaded innocence."

"What do you think?" she asked.

"I think he's a liar, and I should pay him a visit."

"No," Al chimed in. "You're drunk, and you can't just go in without a plan. You'll get hurt."

"I'm fine. I was just there. Dom fears me. I go in, nice and polite, and ask him pleasantly."

"No, *we* go and ask not-so-politely," Om interjected. "I'm going with you."

"No!" Al grabbed my wrist. "Think. This is a bad plan. No, it's not even a plan. You need to plan this out."

I yanked my arm out of his grasp. "Normally, I would agree. Make a strategic plan, follow it, and back off if it's going sideways. Today, not so much. Today is about taking the direct path. Today, we go in nice and friendly and gather information."

"Yeah!" Om added.

Al shook his head. "Do you have your comm? Is it fully charged?"

"Yes, and yes," I replied.

"Good, keep it with you. You'll need it."

Om and I arrived at Domineer's offices only to find it locked down.

"Try the buzzer," I suggested.

Om pushed the buzzer. "Pizza delivery."

"Sorry," a voice replied from the intercom. "The building is on security lockdown. No vendors allowed."

"Well, crap," I complained. "We'll just have to find another way in. We can—"

My words were interrupted by an audible crashing next to me. Om stood there, grinning, in front of a smashed glass door.

"You broke shatterproof glass?" I asked.

"I'm hella strong." She grinned.

"Well, okay! Let's go say hello."

"Let's," Om agreed.

"Crap."

"What?"

"I just realized I'm going in fresh," I answered. "That's all."

"Fresh?"

"Got no powers. They pretty much wore out."

"Oh, is that a problem?"

"Not really. Here, hold my comm." I handed it to Om.

"Why?"

"Because I asked you to. Hide it. Keep it safe."

"Okay."

"These guys might get stupid," I explained. "Don't be a hero. If they break out anything nasty, just duck behind something until I reset."

"Nasty?" Om asked. "Nasty, like what?"

"I don't know, a rocket launcher? You know, something big and ugly. Use your freaking judgment. If it can disintegrate you, duck until I get boosted and take them out."

"So, are we some kind of team now?"

"Are you shitting me?"

Om laughed. "Just checking that you didn't go crazy yet."

"No, not yet."

We entered Chez Dom as if we owned the place.

The security guard stood up to stop us. Before he could even reach his gun, Om punched him in the face. He slumped unconscious in his chair. Om disarmed him.

"Nice." I nodded.

"Thanks." Om smiled sweetly.

The decor in the lobby hadn't changed since my last visit. Still tacky and gaudy to the maximum.

Om scanned the place and sneered. "Gross, it looks like a whore house in here."

"A yup."

We got in the elevator and took it to the top floor. Dom and his cronies were waiting.

"Why are you here?" he asked. "We agreed you would not return."

"You're a goddamn liar."

"I told you before—"

"Yeah, yeah. You didn't send RoboBash, but you hold the leash to the fucker that did." I threw the picture of David on his desk. "Your monkey, your circus, and it came to my town."

Dom picked up the picture and glanced at it. "Yeah, he works for one of our subsidiaries. I believe in one of the real estate divisions."

"Why are your realtors screwing with me?"

"You're so egocentric. It's not always about you."

"What is it about, then?" I asked.

"Chaos, of course. Chaos, terror, and property values. But I'm not behind it."

"Who is?"

He shrugged. "I don't bother with the minutiae. As long as they remain profitable, it's not my problem."

"Yeah," Om said. "Funny how that works."

"What's this?" Dom motioned to Om. "Your intern?"

"Something like that," I answered.

"Well, good. She'll learn a valuable lesson tonight."

"Yeah? What's that? How to wear metallic prints like a geriatric pimp?"

"No," Dom laughed. "She'll learn what your boyfriend taught us. We don't have to kill you. We just have to keep you under. As long as we don't kill you, we can do whatever we want to you." Dom pulled a tranq gun from his desk.

"Run!" Om shouted. But it was too late.

Chapter 8

I awoke strapped to a chair.

"I don't know why nobody thought of this before," Dom said.

"They did," I replied. "It didn't work out so well for them."

"I imagine you ran your big mouth off to the point of taunting them into killing you. We'll take care of that. Bruno, her tongue."

A goon I assumed to be Bruno stepped forward. He pried my mouth open, yanked my tongue with one hand, and with the other, started cutting it off with a small hacksaw. I could feel every muscle fiber ripping. Blood splattered everywhere. The pain was blinding. My screams filled the room.

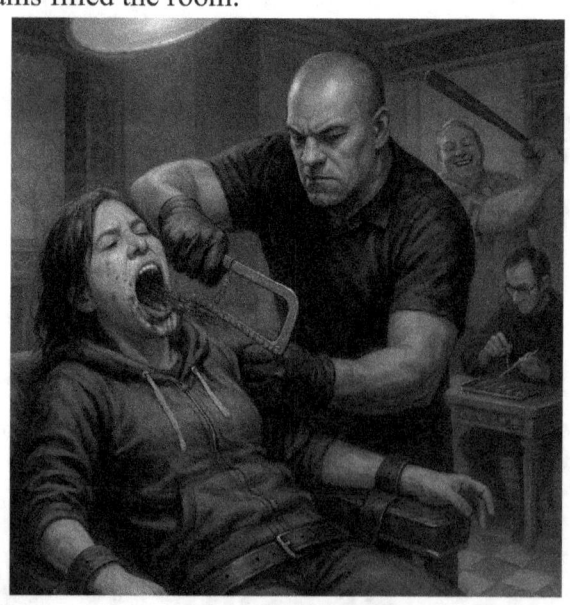

"That should take care of that. Do what you want to her, but keep her alive. Oh, and leave one eye so she can see everything coming."

They went to work. Bruno, Chuck, and Bin cackled as they started the vivisection. Chuck enjoyed inflicting blunt trauma. He danced as he swung his baseball bat into my arms and legs. The first impact was to my right elbow. It struck with a resounding crunch. Shocks of pain shot up through my arm, followed by numbness. He swung the bat over his head in a flourish. However, his swing lacked any finesse, and his form was terrible. I was reasonably confident that he'd never actually played baseball before.

Next, he went for my knees. The first one didn't break immediately. It popped slightly. Chuck remedied that. He struck full force. The knee shattered on impact. I howled in agony, and he laughed. The second knee broke right away. Having had my knees busted at least a half dozen times in the past, I could safely say he rated above average on the pain-dispensing scale. If I had control of my hand, I might have given Chuck a thumbs-up for a job well done. Fortunately, my cries of anguish were enough to amuse the trio.

Chuck went on for about twenty minutes, dancing and pummeling. He got so into it that he slipped and connected with my head. It made a loud crack, and I blacked out for a moment. It was a pleasant break from the pain.

"What did I tell you?" Bruno screamed at Chuck. "The boss said to keep her alive. Caving in her cranium is going to put her lights out. Knock it off! Besides, it's Bin's turn. Let him work off some of that energy."

Bin was really into knives. He spun, flipped, and threw them; I could have sworn he kissed one. I giggled at the thought that he probably slept with them under his pillow as he masturbated to the ninja supply catalog. He ignored my laughter or didn't notice it in his enthusiasm for cutting me. Starting on my arms, he sliced lines and patterns from my shoulders to my wrists. He expertly avoided major veins or arteries. Then he moved on to my torso, cutting up my chest with unbridled joy. He took great pleasure in mutilating me.

"Free boob jobs," Bin announced.

I managed to roll my eyes at his corniness.

"Wait, stop," Chuck said. "We need to sterilize the area." He pulled out a spray bottle and doused me with alcohol. They both giggled as I flinched and squirmed from the added discomfort.

"Hey," Bruno said. "Check this out." He stepped forward, holding a cup of water and a lighter. "Spray her again."

Chuck sprayed me with alcohol, and then Bruno lit me on fire. They watched me burn, taking turns spraying me to ensure the flames didn't go out. When they thought I had had enough, they poured the water on me.

I wept and whimpered, much to their delight. It dawned on me that these fuckers might be even more twisted in the head than I was.

"I think she's giving you the stink eye," Chuck said.

"I'll fix that," Bin replied. He grabbed me by the face and proceeded to gouge my eye out. I tried to think of a quip to amuse myself. Still, it was demoralizing to lose half my sight, even knowing it was temporary. My obvious torment provided the three ample satisfaction. They clapped and laughed. Chuck did a new celebratory dance, and the three started playing catch with my eyeball.

Bruno liked the hacksaw. He sliced off my fingers, one by one. Luckily, I was already numb from the broken bones. If I could speak, I might have mentioned they should reverse the order of the torture next time.

Bruno moved on to my toes, but I didn't respond enough. So, he cut off my left ear. He was thrilled with my squirming and moans. He held it up to my face. "Can you hear me?" he asked.

Yeah, I could hear him and began considering options for future payback.

Chuck held up one of my fingers. "Hey, Bruno, something's wrong with this girl, but I just can't put my finger on it."

"Let me see that," Bruno replied. He grabbed my severed finger and held it to my face. "Look who's giving the finger now. Wait." Bruno giggled. "Check this out," Bruno shoved the finger into my nostril. "Stop picking your nose."

Chuck grabbed a set of pliers and pried my jaw open. I didn't have the strength to offer much resistance. He ripped out two of my front teeth. It wasn't like I hadn't lost more than my share in bar fights alone. However, it still hurt, and I howled in pain.

"Chuck, keep holding her mouth," Bruno said. Chuck continued to grip my face as Bruno peed into my mouth. "Always wanted a portable toilet."

I choked on his urine, feeling like I was drowning. This was almost worse than the time I got waterboarded with day-old borscht. Bruno finished relieving himself and did a small victory strut around the room. Chuck released my jaw, and I coughed out the pee, catching my breath just in time for Bin to jab a pen into my right ear, puncturing my eardrum.

It went on like that for hours. Intense agony, followed by humiliation. They sliced and cut, jammed, and jabbed. I was burned, branded, and waterboarded. Peed on, slapped, kicked, and punched. I lost count of the number of teeth they yanked out. The only thing getting me through it was the knowledge that it would eventually stop, and I would destroy these fuckers. It couldn't go on forever.

"This one is done for the night," Bruno said to his cohorts. "Much more, and she'll go into shock. Let her rest, and we'll play in the morning."

They left the room. I was thankful for the quiet. Despite the pain, I didn't panic. I reminded myself that I had been in worse situations. I always made it out. This was my thing. They always slipped, and a little too much of this or that, I reset. I sat and breathed, centering myself, or what was left of me, when I thought I heard something. I could have sworn there was crashing and yelling in the distance. But everything went silent again. I was in no shape to count on any of my senses.

The door opened. "E?"

"Olm."

"Holy crap." Om winched. "What did they do to you?" She untied me from the chair.

"Ooop me."

"What?" Om asked.

"Ooop me!"

"Shoot you? I can't."

"Oo ii!"

Om pointed her gun at me. She winced as she pulled the trigger.

BAM

Paradise. My friends, Death and the Universe, greeted me and showed me the light, sending me on my way.

Regeneration. My missing body parts reformed, my brain healed, and my nerves reconnected. I was pleased I didn't have to see it. The ordeal must have been gruesome, because Om's face writhed in repulsion.

More pain. Plus, some itching from my still healing appendages and that lovely feeling of being made out of rock.

I came fully to, diamond coated.

"That sucked," Om said.

"No shit. How did you escape?"

"The door just opened," Om replied. "They threw me in a locked room until they decided what to do with me. I had your comm hidden like you said. When I knew they weren't watching, I tried to call out. It wouldn't do anything like it was bricked. I gave up, but after a couple hours, it started acting weird, flashing and stuff. Then the door just opened."

"Thank you, big guy."

"You're thanking God?" Om asked.

"No, someone better. Give me my comm."

Om handed it to me. "How are we going to get out of here?"

"Very carefully."

"You mean like how we came in?"

I didn't answer her right away. Instead, I sent an encrypted text to Al. Within seconds, the power to the entire building went down.

"I mean like that. The bad news is we need to take the stairs."

"I can use the exercise," Om said.

"I need to make one stop, and then we're out."

"Stop?" Om asked. "Where?

"You didn't happen to see where Bruno, Chuck, and Bin went, would you?"

Om grinned. "No, but I grabbed this." Om held up a portable interoffice comm. "Should I power it on?"

"Oh, yeah."

She turned on the comm, and we followed the chatter. Eventually, through the chaos, Bruno instructed Bin to meet him by the southeast third-floor stairwell.

"I need to adjust some attitudes." I grinned. "It may get ugly."

"If it gets too gross, I won't watch."

"That's my girl. Let's go."

We scrambled to the stairwell. We could hear Bruno's crew below us. Adrenaline took over. I charged down the stairs toward them and heard Om behind me.

Bruno, Chuck, and Bin took advantage of the power outage to duck out of work. I found them in the back of the landing in a small alcove meant to store custodial supplies. They sat around a small card table in folding chairs, drinking and playing cards.

"What a fucking pathetic yet stereotypical display." I sauntered over. "You lazy shitbags."

"How is she up?" Bruno asked.

"I didn't do it," Chuck replied.

"I know you dumbasses didn't do it. You were with me, but someone let her out." Bruno pointed at me. "Why are you walking?"

"Are you that stupid?" I asked. "You must have done internal damage, which killed me."

"If you were dead," Chuck said. "You wouldn't be standing here."

"Yes," I replied. "Yes, you are that stupid."

"Let me put her down," Chuck said. "I'll make sure I do it right."

"I've been thinking about this," I said. "I could take the high road, smack you around a little, and hope you learn a lesson. Or I go with my gut and simply kill you. You keep asking me to kill you, but you're also mentally challenged. So, what do I do? I guess I'll have to take the middle ground."

Chuck sneered and came at me with his aluminum bat. He hit me square in the head, the bat bent around my skull. I grabbed it and swung. I took out Chuck's knees. He fell to the ground, whimpering.

Bin came at me with his pretty knife. He must have been especially challenged. He didn't learn from Chuck's attack. He tried to plunge the blade into my chest. It deflected off me, confusing Bin thoroughly. I punched him in the arm, causing him to drop the blade. I picked it up and stabbed him in the left eye. He screamed and collapsed. I reclaimed the knife from his eye socket. He clutched his face, sobbing.

I smiled at Bruno. He tried to run. There was no place to go. I took him to the ground and went to work. It took a lot of effort, but I managed to get his tongue.

"That, my friends, is accelerated Karma. Learn from this, or I might come back."

I turned to find Om at the base of the stairs. "Are you done being crazy?" she asked. "Can we go now?"

"You saw. Those asshats had it coming."

"You have a serious impulse control problem."

"What?" I asked. "I could have killed them."

Om shook her head. "Wow."

We took off down an annoying, lengthy labyrinth of stairs. When we hit the ground floor, armed security personnel were waiting. Fortunately, we remained unseen in the chaos. We ducked back into the stairwell.

"Shit, damn, fuck!" I cursed.

"Ass," Om added.

"Ass?"

"You used the good ones."

"I could have come up with at least six others."

"No doubt." Om rolled her eyes. "What now?"

"Can't risk the straightforward approach. You could get fragged."

"Then what?"

"One sec." I sent a text to Al. "Pinned down ground level, right, rear, stairwell. Help."

"Told you it was a bad idea," he texted back.

Suddenly, an explosion rang out from the basement. Most of the security agents ran to the basement stairwell and out of sight. The few that remained would be easy to outrun. We took off. Om was pretty fast, but I was able to match her pace. We dashed out of the same hole we made to get in.

We ran for blocks until we were sure we were not being followed.

"What was that?" Om asked.

"I don't know. I think we'll find out at home."

———∿∿∿———

When we returned home, Al was furious.

"Sit!" He pointed at the sofa. We both complied.

"What exploded?" I asked.

"A hot water heater," Al answered. "They make a loud noise when they go. You were lucky the building even had one."

"How?" Om asked. "Who?"

"Al, you don't think they could trace you?" I inquired.

Al shook his head. "I don't know. They won't know who did it, but they might know someone got in."

"Oops," I said.

"Oops? You should have known better!" He pointed at me. "And you." He motioned to Om. "I'm fairly certain you should have known better, too."

"I'm sorry." I winced as I digested his words. I hated that he was right again. "I was feeling so pumped and got swept up in the moment."

"Do you always get like this after you recover from stacking, all rainbows and butterflies?"

"I am not 'all rainbows and butterflies'. Are you insinuating that I'm perky?"

"Compared to your normal morose self, yeah. You're the only person I know who actually gets off from being killed. It's like you enjoy suffering. Maybe the torture will keep you buzzed out for the next week."

"You were tortured," Al's voice was barely audible.

"Thanks, Om," I glared at her. "Al, I'm okay."

"Oops," Om said.

"I didn't wait decades for you just to have you throw your life away in a manic, drunken rampage."

I clutched his face with both hands and kissed him where his mouth should be. "I'll be more careful. No more drunken missions."

"You will be my death," he replied.

"Ew," Om complained. "Wait until I leave before you start your elder junk."

I sat back down on the sofa next to Om. "Do I look old to you?"

"You don't look it, but I know you're like some old cat lady under it all."

"I got nothing," I replied.

Al came to my rescue. "What did you learn from your impromptu investigation?"

"Getting your tongue cut out hurts," I replied. "A lot."

"Eris is completely insane," Om stated.

Al clutched his temples. "Did you learn anything useful?"

"Not much. The Dom guy said something about chaos, terror, and property values. Did you read the Carnal Max stuff?"

"Yeah," I said. "It's pretty abstract. I had to read it three times just to understand it. But it takes place on this multidimensional plane, where Carnal Max, a man reborn from the tears and blood of his slain family, battles Boss Doom, the leader of the black-blood army. Doom was hell-bent on using the poor for fuel and food. It's really gory and depressing. Max has a magic jar by his front door that he uses to leave his soul in before battle to protect it from evil. He discovers Boss Doom's plan to scare all the poor people out of one of the dimensional planes so he can turn it into a playground for his followers. So, Boss Doom pays criminals to rampage and kill the poor. Then he rounds up the survivors and sticks them in pens to kill and use as raw materials to power his pleasure palace. Carnal Max tries to free them but keeps getting defeated. It was a horrific comic book."

"That is odd," Om said. "Nothing very helpful there."

"No, wait," I replied. "The jar."

"What jar?" Om asked.

"The jar in the comic. There was a jar at Max's cabin. It was the only thing that was not basic furniture."

"They had to have grabbed it when they cleaned out the place," Om said.

"Maybe not. It got knocked over when I kicked Keen's gun away. It could have rolled out of sight."

"That is if they didn't burn the place down," Om said.

"Do you know where the cabin was? I wasn't very aware when we dropped from the plane… or afterward."

"Yeah, I have the location."

"Al," I asked. "Did they burn the place down?"

Om showed Al the location on a GPS map.

Al sat quietly for a moment. "The cabin has been burned down," he reported. "However, there is some debris left behind."

"You know this how?" Om asked. "Never mind." She held up her hand. "I don't want to know. Well, it's worth a check."

"We can get a rental and head out there. Al, want to come with or monitor remotely?"

"I'll monitor," Al replied. "Can I trust you to be careful?"

"Yes," I answered. "No doubt we've rattled some cages with our friendly visit."

"No doubt," Al agreed. "Onyx, please hand me your comm."

Om handed it to him. He held it for less than a second and returned it to her.

"Keep it with you," he said.

Om nodded.

"Could you search the area while we're traveling?" I asked. "Maybe you can give us some ideas of where to start."

"Yes. Please check in from time to time," Al said.

"Can't you track us?" I asked.

Al nodded. "But I would still like to hear your voice."

I couldn't stop the grin. "You got it, aibee."

Part 3: An ounce of discretion is worth a pound of shit.

Chapter 9

It would be a twenty-hour drive if we didn't have to stop. By the time we completed our transaction at the rental kiosk, the sun was up. Om and I decided to break the drive into five-hour blocks. I took the first shift.

We made our rest stops quick and direct. One of us used the restroom while the other watched from the parking lot. Food was a grab-and-go affair from whatever was pre-made. We were heavily armed, so we drove the speed limit and stayed in the right lane. I checked in with Al on the hour. We made the drive in nineteen hours and twenty-two minutes. I parked in a nearby nature reserve. We would have to walk the remaining five kilometers.

"You ready?" I asked Om.

She nodded and crammed down the last bite of her gas station burrito.

"Let's do it."

We arrived at the cabin before sunrise. I pulled out my flashlight and began to search the rubble. We searched by quadrants, each taking opposite ends. Everything we found was thrown into plastic bags. Clad in long sleeves, rubber gloves, and hairnets, we left nothing to chance. By the time the sun had fully risen, we'd scanned every centimeter of the site.

"Well, that's it. Fuck if we missed anything." I did a final check around the site.

"Yup." Om shook her head.

"Tired?" I asked.

"A little, but it's okay."

"Me, too. Let's get the fuck home."

We began the long drive back. Again, I took the first shift.

"Well, whatever was in this jar is gone," Om lamented. "It's in at least six pieces."

"Not necessarily," I replied. "Who says there isn't something embedded in it?"

"Ah." Om grinned. "Good thinking. That's why you're a captain."

"No," I laughed. "I was a captain because I had all the educational requirements and took any training that was offered. As long as you stick to the plan, you get rank."

"You didn't like the military?"

I shrugged. "I liked it enough. It was fine until I became the superhero poster girl, you know?"

"I think so." Om nodded. "You didn't like being a mascot."

"Yes! Yes! You fucking got it. I think you and maybe Al are the only ones who understand. So, where did you learn to draw like that?"

"Oh, I was always artsy," Om answered. "I've been going to school on and off for graphic design. For a while, I was a tattoo artist. I also know my way around a bar."

"Yeah, Al told me. I tried to convince him to have you open the other day."

"Because you didn't want to get out of bed?"

"I really didn't want to get out of bed."

"Really? Why?"

I just grinned.

"Oh, gross."

"You asked," I said.

"I'm sorry I did. Call Al."

"Oh yeah, 'call Al.'" My comm connected to Al.

"Where are you?" he asked.

"On the highway," I replied. "But you know that. We're on our way home."

"Good, keep checking in so I know you're safe."

"We're fine," I said. Just then, a vehicle pulled out from the shoulder and t-boned us. "Crap!"

"Are you okay?"

"No, Al, we're under attack," Om shouted. "Monitor us."

I grabbed a weapon from the back seat. Om followed my lead.

Two men in poor-fitting gray suits jumped out of the vehicle that struck us. I aimed my weapon at one of them.

"Give us what you have," one said. "Give it to us, and there will be no trouble."

"We don't have anything," I replied. "Back off."

"Funny, our video surveillance saw you picking through private property, putting stuff in bags."

"I have no idea what you're talking about," Om stated. "Please leave."

The second guy took a step toward us. "Don't make this hard."

"Oh," I replied. "I will make this brutal."

The first guy launched some kind of plasma ball from his hand. It gained size as it closed the distance to us. "Stall," I told Om as I jumped into it.

It felt like I was hit with napalm. I could feel my skin melt and flake off. It wasn't the quick death that I hoped for. Then again, it never was.

When I hit paradise, the universe greeted me with a smile. "Off you go," she said. Death waved at me as the universe bathed me in her light.

I regained my bodily control in mere moments. Om was ducked behind the car, exchanging fire with the assailants. I got up and approached the pair.

The second guy launched a fire attack. Jets of flame extended from his fingers. Fortunately, my new plasma defense was sufficient enough to block the firestorm. I stepped up and punched him in the throat.

He fell to the ground, choking and coughing. He wouldn't die, but he'd be hurting for a couple of weeks. I turned to the first guy and kicked him in the kneecap. He collapsed to the ground screaming.

"See?" I shouted to Om. "This is what happens when you depend on your tweaks too much."

"But you just…" Om shook her head. "Never mind. Let's get out of here."

"Will the vehicle go?"

Om started the vehicle. It was running… barely.

Lights approached in the distance. I jumped in the passenger seat. "Gun it!"

Om complied. She sped off onto the highway as fast as our broken rental would allow. A vehicle sped up from behind and rear-ended us.

"Al, you there?" I yelled into my comm. "What's chasing us?"

"Besides the one on your bumper, you have four vehicles in pursuit," he replied. "Each has four people inside."

"Can we take them?"

"No."

"Death from above?" I asked.

"Death from above." Al agreed.

"Death from above?" Om screamed. "What the hell is death from above?"

"They are all converging on the next exit," Al said. "One is coming in the opposite direction. Get beyond that vehicle, and you'll be clear."

"You heard the man, Om. Can you get us clear?"

"Do I have a choice?" Om hit the gas, and the vehicle started to vibrate violently. A set of headlights approached from the opposite direction. They hit the median and spun around behind us. Now, one vehicle was trying to run us off the road from the side while the other slammed us from the back.

"Om, go faster," I implored.

"This is as fast as it will go. There's speed inhibitors on these rentals."

"Al!"

"Got it," he said. "Sync up your comm with the car's systems." I pushed the quick pair button, and Al linked to the vehicle.

A moment later, I was thrown back in my seat as the vehicle accelerated at an alarming rate.

"Whoo, yeah!" Om yelled as she forced the ailing vehicle to attain speeds it was never meant to achieve. The shaking was terrifying, but it was nothing compared to what was to come.

"Don't look behind you," I instructed Om.

"Are you shitting me?" She gripped the steering wheel tighter and glanced back.

"I said not to look, didn't…"

That's when the flaming ball of death careened overhead. It struck the highway behind us, shaking the road and sending a shockwave into the vehicle. I saw Om fight the wheel, barely keeping us on the road. The sound of the explosion was overwhelming. I screamed but heard nothing but the deafening rumbling.

Then, suddenly, there was complete silence. I panted, fighting to catch my breath. Om was paler than I had ever seen her, gripping the wheel for dear life.

Slowly, sound began to return. I heard the noise of the engine screaming in protest. Then Om started laughing.

"Death from above, holy crap. Was that a satellite?"

"A small one," I replied. "I think. Al, you there?"

"Yes," he answered.

"Are we still being pursued?"

"You're not."

"Where should we meet?"

"I'll send you coordinates."

"Al," Om yelled. "You're amazing!"

"No," I corrected her. "Al's better than that."

We met in a motel in a small, suburban town away from the highway.

Al brought healthy snacks, empanadas, egg rolls, and coffee.

We ate in virtual silence, Om and I shoved food down like we'd never eaten before. After the bounty was devoured, Om fumbled around for more.

"That's it?" Om pulled up a napkin, checking the space underneath for any missed crumbs.

"Sorry, I think I ate one of your empanadas. I was hungry as fuck."

Om shrugged. "It's cool. I saw a bodega down the street. I'll go restock."

"Bodega, hmmm." I grinned. "Go, New York! Grab some cash coins from my pocket."

"I got it," Om winked and patted her pocket. "Bronx."

"Stretch your legs. Take your time."

The door slammed behind her.

I stood. "So aibee, we have at least a half-an-hour. Whatcha wanna do?"

Al cocked his head. "What did you have in mind?"

I pulled off my shirt and then unbuttoned my pants.

Al sat motionless for a moment. "Keep going," he growled.

I wiggled out of my pants and sauntered over to Al. Leaning over him, I exhaled onto his neck. He reached behind my back with one hand and unhooked my bra. Then he wrapped his arm around my waist and pulled me onto his lap.

I reached my hands under his shirt and began stroking his surface. "Take it all off," I breathed.

He moaned and pulled off his shirt. Sucking and licking my way downward, I unfastened his pants. He squirmed as I ran my tongue along the waistband.

"Want more?" I asked. "I want to make you scream." Reaching to the floor, I poked through my pants pocket and pulled out the sensor stimulator. But as I went to deploy it, Al grabbed my arm.

"Not that," he groaned. "Just you."

"Okay," I smirked. "We'll keep the tech out of this. Take me to bed."

Al stood, swept me into his arms, and carried me to the closest bed.

"Give it to me, you sexy metal beast."

After shedding the remainder of our clothes, Al and I wrapped ourselves around each other.

I swam in his body, taking long, deep strokes, coming up for air only after each wave of pleasure. He writhed around, seemingly completely out of control of his functions. I refused to let up, riding him repeatedly into ecstasy.

"I wanna go all night," I gasped.

Al regained control of his functions and rolled me over on my back. He ran his hands over my breasts, then downward. I whimpered as he began stroking me.

"I want to feel you," I gasped. "All of you."

Al climbed up on me and we intertwined. We treaded the waters of euphoria, each wave bringing us deeper into rapture.

"So, good, so—"

The door burst open. "Scored more empanadas!"

Om gawked at our naked forms and dropped the bag. She ran to the bathroom and slammed the door.

"I told you to take your time," I yelled.

"I was gone an hour," she shouted from the bathroom. "An hour!"

"Oops." I giggled. "We lost track of time."

Om didn't respond.

"Om?" I jumped up and threw on my clothes. "Are you okay?"

Still no response.

Al dressed himself and stepped up to the door. He knocked gently. "Onyx. Please speak with us."

After a few moments of silence, the bathroom door opened, and Om stepped out. She walked past Al and sat at the small table in the corner. I grabbed the bag of food and settled into the chair beside her, placing it on the table. Al joined us.

"Sorry." Om frowned. "Flashback."

I nodded. "I think I understand. Your mother?"

"Yeah," Om slumped in her seat. "I walked in on her more than a few times. It never got easier. Straight to the bathroom. That was the rule."

"Ew. You would think your mother would plan so you wouldn't have to see anything."

"She didn't plan anything." A tear ran down her cheek. "She was going for an abortion when they gave her other options."

"Oh, no." I gasped.

"When she decided to keep me, you know, for the money, she kept an apartment for a few months but then went back to crappy motels to save money for other things."

"Other things being cocaine?" I asked.

Om nodded. "And anything else she could get high off of. She just liked coke best."

"Wow." I found myself at a loss for words.

"We should have been more careful," Al said. "Please accept my apology."

"No," Om replied. "Your geriatric sexploits are gross, but my mother isn't your fault. I tried to be good. Barely made it through school. I really wanted to be something better than her."

"You are much better than her." I squeezed Om's hand. "Considering your parenting, you did amazing."

"So, your parents weren't that bad?"

I grinned. "My parents were very cool. They tweaked me because of some genetic damage my mom got hit with during the Trusk offensive. I own my fuck ups, well, mostly. Let me rephrase that, I own my childhood fuck ups."

Om smirked. "How about you, Al?"

"Ji-hoon." Al paused in contemplation. "He was a brilliant AI architect, a mediocre electrical engineer, a compassionate parent, and a complete pervert."

"Why?" Om asked.

"Why was he a pervert?" I laughed. "Because he built Al with a ton of sex sensors."

"Ji-hoon liked the ladies. He wanted me to like them, too."

"Luckily, Al got me to tweak him now. And I'm a far better engineer."

"And just as much of a pervert." Al pointed at the stimulator on the floor.

"I only wanted to make you feel good, fartknocker." I retrieved the stimulator and put it in my pocket. "So it doesn't fall into the wrong hands."

"Sounds like your hands are the wrong ones," Om stated. "What does that thing do?"

"I push it against a sensor and instant orgasm."

"Ew! That's creepy."

"See," Al added. "Onyx thinks it's creepy."

"Okay. I get it." I nodded. "Maybe. It's probably for the best that Ji-hoon and I never got together to plot."

"He was fascinated with you," Al said.

"Ji-hoon? Why? We only met once, I think."

"Yes. And you made quite the impression." Al turned to Om. "She entered the bar and said, 'Hey, aibee, you look dangerous. How about you show me what you can do with a bottle?'"

Om laughed and wiped the tears from her face.

I grinned.

"I remember that. It was the second time we met. I had just got back from...a thing. That was a good shot, too. You're an excellent bartender."

"You left Ji-hoon slack-jawed. I've never seen anyone or anything have that impact on him. He upped the sensor installation after that."

"See. We made Ji-hoon's dream come true." I winked at Al.

"Wait," Om interjected. "Al, your own father rebuilt your body."

"Well, yes and no," I replied.

"I was asking Al," Om turned to Al. "You're some hacker or something. So, how do you do that? Death from above and everything?"

"We know each other well," Al replied.

"We are in sync," I added.

"Oh, I just saw that," Om stated. "But you know what I mean. How exactly do you do all that stuff, Al? What are you?"

I looked at Al, not sure what he wanted to reveal.

"Your call, aibee. Om knows most of my story."

Al hesitated briefly, "I can interface and control systems."

"What kind of systems?" Om asked.

"Anything connected to a network."

"Whoa, just how much of you is replaced? I just saw you naked. You have no... um, actual flesh."

I looked at Al, and he glanced back at me.

"You're completely artificial?" Om asked. "What about your brain?"

"I never had a brain," Al answered. "Not as you would understand one."

"Wait, you're a…"

"He's an AI," I answered.

"Holy crap! That's so cool," Om said. "And nobody knows?"

"You know," Al said. "Eris knows. My nephew, Boy, and my lawyer know. Some government agencies know."

"You have a nephew?"

"Al's father is Boy's grandfather," I explained.

"Your father, Ji-hoon, the man who made you. The guy who has his picture posted in Spaz."

"Yes," Al answered.

"Oh, you weren't kidding when you said complicated."

"Did you ever get hold of Boy, Al?" I asked.

"No," he replied. "I tried him several times before we became occupied. I only got his personal message box. I left messages."

"He didn't call back?"

"No… he must be busy."

"I disagree. Boy should have called back. Did you try the lawyer? He'll always answer. Any call could be coin."

"I can try now," Al said. "The office should be open now. He keeps night hours."

Al put his personal comm on speaker and called. The call went straight to the message box.

"That can't be right," I said. "Do you have Legal's personal comm?"

Al called, and it also went to the message box.

"Hack it," I said.

"Hack what?" Al asked.

"Whatever is redirecting the calls to the message box. Hack it."

"What makes you think it's redirected?" Al asked.

"Because I know they wouldn't blow you off. Something's wrong. Besides, what lawyer would ignore potential business opportunities?"

"One moment." Al sat still for a moment. "You're correct."

"Really?" I asked.

"Yes. There's a program intentionally forcing all calls into message boxes and deleting the messages."

"Can you bypass it?"

"I believe I can," Al answered. "You sleep when I work on it."

"What about you," Om asked.

"I don't need to sleep," Al stated.

"You should back up," I said.

"I will. But you two have been awake for too long. You should sleep first."

"Okay, sleepy time. Come on, Om." I stripped down to my underwear and jumped into one of the beds. Om took the other. "Wake us if you get hold of Boy or Legal. Shit, wake us even if the smallest thing happens."

"Agreed."

At first, my sleep was restless because of the evening's death. But the exhaustion was severe enough to knock me out hard. When Al woke me up, it was still dark.

"How long did I sleep?" I asked.

"Three hours," he answered.

"Is everything okay?"

"Yes, I think I can get through to Legal now."

"Oh, shit." I looked around the room. "Is the girl asleep?"

"She is."

"Should we wake her?" I asked.

"I'm awake now," Om mumbled.

"We're calling Legal."

Om sat up in her bed and faced us.

I rolled upright and patted the bed next to me. Al sat. "I'm going to attempt a vidcomm," he said.

Al pointed to the vidcomm projection against the wall and initiated the call.

"...coming in! Gotta get it." Gary Legal's face appeared on the feed.

"Good evening," Al greeted.

"Al!" Legal's face lifted into a huge grin. "How you doing, buddy?"

"I'm well," Al replied. "How are you?"

"We're fine here, just a little busy."

"Should I call you later?" Al asked.

"NO!" I yelled. "We need to talk to him, nimrod."

"Who's that?" Gary squinted. "Wait, do I know you?"

"That is my girlfriend, Eris," Al replied.

"Whoa, buddy!" Legal exclaimed. "You know how to pick 'em. I know you." He pointed at me. "If you ever need representation, which is inevitable, I'm your guy."

"Thank you," I replied. "I'll keep that in mind. So, is everything okay over there?"

"Everything is just great," Legal replied. He shifted nervously.

"How's Boy?" I asked.

"Boy is fine, just fine. He's out attending a social protest."

"What kind of social protest?" Al asked.

"Just…" Gary's words were interrupted by the sound of a large explosion. The feed flickered. "That," he said.

"What exactly is going on there?" I asked. "Don't tell me it's fine or okay because from what I see, something's jacked up."

Legal frowned. "It's ugly here. These real estate relocators keep shipping people in and dropping them in what they call 'planned communities,' but they're just work camps."

"What?" I reached over and grabbed the Outer Colony brochure that Om and I were given. "The realtors are convincing people to sell their crap and leave. Look at this shit." I held up the brochure for Gary to see.

"Yeah." He nodded. "That's consistent with what we've been hearing from these poor saps. They're sold a bill of goods but don't check the fine print. The buyers fail to pay the 'port fees' upon arrival and forfeit their contract, leaving them stranded and owing a massive penalty. Then the sorry bastards get shuffled over to civil court, where they're ordered to have their wages garnished or face prison time, so they have to take the first job they can find. A recruiter conveniently is on hand to offer them a factory job until they sort everything out. That job conveniently comes with—" Legal made air quotes. "'Housing'. They shove six people into a one-room shack without power, running water, or sewage. You get the idea. And then we have a whole company store scam going, trapping the poor suckers in a cycle of debt."

"What if they don't get a job?" I asked.

"They get stuck in a prison with eight people to a room and are forced to do heavy labor."

"Okay, what if they have the port fees?"

"Nobody has the port fees," Legal stated. "They seem to know exactly how much coin these people have and charge them just above that."

"Stupid realtors!" Om yelled.

"Al." Legal grinned. "Do you have two girlfriends?"

"I don't," Al replied. "That's Onyx. She had a bad experience with real estate agents."

"Hoo Kay," Legal replied.

"I assume you're providing a legal remedy for these people," Al stated.

"I'm doing my best, buddy. You wouldn't happen to have anything I can use for evidence?"

"Not much," I said. "But we're working on it. We could use any clues you may have."

Legal nodded. "I'll send you what I got. Maybe that will help you."

"Thank you," Al said. "I'll send you anything we find."

"Thank you, man." Gary gave us the thumbs up.

"Please send Boy my love," Al said. "I miss you both."

"We miss you," Legal replied.

"Don't let anything happen to Boy during these protests," I added.

"Are you kidding? He's stubborn like this guy." Legal motioned at Al. "I'll do my best."

"I'll contact you soon," Al said.

"Good," Legal replied. "Do everything I wouldn't do."

The connection dropped, and we sat in silence.

"What's in his files?" I asked.

"Hand me a tab," Al said.

I handed him a news tab. He held it for a moment and handed it back.

"Well, they certainly fucked a shit ton of people."

I looked at page after page of affidavits from homeowners swindled out of their property to be relocated to a work camp.

"It's just like he said. These people were shafted very professionally."

Om looked over my shoulder. "How many pages is that?"

"Thousands," I replied.

"That's ugly," she said. "We have to do something."

"Yup," I agreed. "But not tonight. Let's get some sleep."

"I second that." Om went back to bed and got under the covers.

Al laid down on the bed next to me. I leaned back against him. He started stroking my hair.

"It's fucked up. We finally get our crap together, and I drag us back into the shit."

"I think we needed to be dragged into this one," Al said.

"Really?"

"Yes. You stumbled on something big and are the only one who can fix it."

"No," I replied. "We're the only ones who can fix it."

I woke up wrapped around Al. Om was already awake and watching through the windows.

"...when she is awake," Al was saying.

"I'm up." I sat up and stretched.

"We were saying that you were most likely correct about Max embedding something in the jar. We need to find a place to scan it."

"I don't have anyone anymore."

"I do," Om said.

"Yeah?"

Om held up a community college ID. "I can get into any university student lab."

"You brilliant girl." I grinned. "Al, you can keep watch when we go in. Wait, who's watching the bar?"

"I contacted Sam. He has an emergency key."

"Can you trust him?"

"To keep it in one place, yes. To make money? No. I expect he'll be giving away drinks without hesitation, but that's a loss I have to accept."

"I'll cover it," I said. "You know that."

"Thank you," Al replied.

"I always got your back." I winked at him.

Chapter 10

The closest college was a ten-minute drive from the motel. We pulled into the main gate.

"How may I help you folks?" the security guard asked.

"Oh my God!" Om yelled. "I like totally blanked, and my project is due. It's not like it's my fault if my stupid Da and my…" Om rolled her eyes. "… stepmother hadn't dragged me out on this lame family bonding trip. I would be done already. Tina and Angela were going to remind me to do it after the party. But now, they couldn't remind me since I flaked out on the party. And my grade is going to be completely bogus. I need to scan my jar, or I will fail. Fail! I never failed anything. Please, please, please, save me." Om clutched her hands, pleading. "If I fail, I have to live with them again, and she walks around the house naked. Ew."

The security guard stood there slack-jawed and just waved us in.

I, too, was speechless. We pulled through the gate.

"The laboratories are straight ahead and to the right," Al instructed through the comm. "I believe if we gain access to the medical assistant student laboratory, we can use the sonogram lab to scan the jar safely."

We pulled alongside one of the less visible back doors to the lab. Al hacked into the security system and opened it. Om and I ran inside as fast as we could.

"Which way?" I asked Al.

"To the left, at the end of the hall."

Om and I followed Al's directions. We walked into a small examination room with a sonogram machine. Fortunately, the manual to operate the device was written for college students, making it easy to configure. Soon, we had it calibrated and began scanning the jar.

"There it is," Om said. She took a marker and circled the spot on the jar. "I think it's a crystal drive."

"Can we—"

"Someone's coming," Al interrupted.

Om and I scrambled to find a hiding spot, but there was none.

I jumped on the table and lifted my shirt. Om took my queue and grabbed the transducer probe. The door opened.

"I told you this would happen, you slut," she said.

"I thought if I did it upside down, I wouldn't get pregnant," I replied.

"Excuse me." A very rigid-looking woman in hospital scrubs entered the room. "What are you doing in here?"

"Studying," Om said.

"Mmm, hmmm." The woman crossed her arms. "This room is not a playground. If you need medical attention, I recommend you visit the student infirmary." She pointed at the door behind her.

"Uh, okay," Om said. She put down the transducer and started toward the door. I gathered the bag with the jar and followed. As I passed the woman, she grabbed my arm.

"You can get pregnant in any position. Use birth control."

"Yes." I nodded. "I'll use a sock next time."

Om and I ran down the hallway and out the door. Om was giggling maniacally.

"Sock." She laughed as she jumped in the passenger seat.

"We got something," I explained to Al as we sped off.

"You have something alright," Al replied. "Security is on their way over. You two always find trouble."

We gunned it. After swinging by the motel and picking up Al, I drove further away from the highway and deeper into the suburban jungle. We decided to avoid cities but knew we'd stick out in any place too rural.

A motel in a quiet strip mall town became our new shelter. We ordered room service while Al scanned the crystal drive in the bathroom. A feast was quickly delivered. I tipped the server well so he would be less disposed to mention us to anyone who might come looking.

Om and I had not had a fresh hot meal in over a week. We scarfed down the food like it was our first or maybe our last.

"Mmm," Om moaned between bites of her hamburger. "This has to be the best hamburger I've ever eaten."

"Yeah, I'm starving, too. Food is good." I enjoyed the lousy facsimile of sweet and sour chicken as if it were the real deal.

Al stepped out of the bathroom where he had been working. His demeanor did not strike me as encouraging.

"Have you finished eating," he asked.

"No," I replied. "So, if you have bad news, it has to wait."

Al sat in a chair quietly.

"Fucking shit," I cursed. "What is it?"

"Finish eating," he said.

"Are you kidding me? I can't eat now."

"I can." Om kept feeding her face.

"Tell us already," I demanded.

"I found the data on this drive," he said.

"Excellent!" I gave a thumbs up.

"It's encrypted," Al continued.

"And? Encryption has never been a problem for you before."

"True," he replied. "But I'm not all here."

"What do you mean 'all here'?" Om turned to me. "What does he mean by 'all here'?"

"I mean that I host additional processing abilities remotely. I don't need it for daily activities, but it's normally accessible when I require higher brain functions."

"Okay, so where is it?" Om asked. "Oh no, don't tell me it's at the house or the bar?"

"No, it's not at the house or the bar," Al replied.

"Well, let's go to where it is." Om jumped out of her chair.

"It's not that simple," he said.

"It never is," I sighed.

"I need a satellite uplink," he explained.

"And let me guess," I said. "That's at the house."

"It was," Al replied. "My connection was interrupted after death from above."

"Great." I clutched my temples. "What about the bar?"

"Do you think we can even get in there?" Om asked. "You know that place is being watched by everyone."

"Where else can we get an uplink?" I asked.

"A vid station," Om replied

"Heh." I grinned. "Maybe we should pay Brad and Lucy a visit."

"You would rather break into a vidfeed station than go to his own bar?" Om asked.

"Well, you were the one who said we would never get in there." I looked at Al. "Where do you think we have a better chance?"

The parking lot of the vid station was practically empty. The station was an old, nondescript building that resembled an old-timey house. It was a vinyl-sided nightmare that looked like one gust of wind away from collapsing. Vid stations didn't get the funding they used to. The pay net had virtually replaced their function. It was a miracle that the place was still running at all.

We parked in a discreet corner, partially concealed by a bush and a dumpster. After a few hours of watching the traffic flow in and out of the place, it looked like the last of the swing shift was leaving, and the night staff was shuffling in. Fortunately, the night shift was thin. Most of the programming was preset and needed minimal attention.

"So, you just need to plug into those dishes, right?" Om asked.

"No," Al replied. "I need to connect to the transmitter feed inside."

"Any idea where the feed is?" I asked.

"There are several possibilities," Al explained. "But I found the backup uplink, which should draw less attention while I'm connected."

"Well, let's use that one," Om said.

"The problem is—"

"Why is there always a problem with you?" I asked. "Why don't you ever say, let's do this, and it will be easy?"

"If it were easy, anyone could do it," Al stated.

"That's not a real answer, nimrod." I smacked him on the head.

"Hey," Om interjected. "It's not his fault."

"You stay out of this. He's not your man."

"He's not yours either," Om replied. "You told me at the bus stop."

"Well, that changed."

"Sure, whatever, you just keep going back and forth with that," Om said.

"I do not. Al wasn't my man before. Now he is. What the fuck?"

"Oh, okay, so only when it's convenient for you?"

"No," I replied. "Let me clarify. The bus stop conversation was pre-banging. You and I got home. Shit happened. Then Al and I fucked. Now we're together. Are we clear?"

Al looked away, avoiding eye contact with either of us.

"You have to be the crudest person I've ever met," Om stated. "Al, how do you put up with her?"

"She has her advantages," he replied.

"Holy crap!" Om yelled. "You two are freaks."

"Everyone's a freak," Al stated. "Each in his own way."

"Yeah, yeah, very deep. How the fuck do we get to the uplink?"

"We have to get through the offices," Al explained. "It's the only way to access it. And that requires us getting through security."

"They have security?" I asked. "In this dive?"

"Don't let the building fool you," Al replied. "They have their share of stalkers and fanatics."

"Well, poop," Om cursed. "How are we going to get in?"

"Can we socially engineer them?" I asked. "Om has a thing."

"My thing only makes people talk to me about themselves. It doesn't make them do stuff. How about Al?"

"Not likely," Al stated. "I won't blend in. Unless you go in without me."

"You're the whole reason we're here," I said. "You have to go in."

"How long do you need to connect?" Om asked. "How long will it take?"

"Once I connect, I'll need at least two minutes, maybe three. I'll transmit the data from the crystal drive to my remote processors, decrypt it, and download it to a new crystal drive."

"How long to get connected?"

"It should only take a moment."

"So, we're taking five minutes?" I asked.

"Yes." Al nodded. "That should be sufficient time."

"Okay, where in the building is the uplink? Please tell me it's in an outer room?"

"The uplink's in that corner." Al pointed at the left corner in front of us.

"There's a small window there," Om said. "Maybe we can break through that."

"Al will never get his fat ass through that."

"I'm not fat," Al objected. "I don't even eat."

"He's big-boned," Om stated.

"Well, big'un," I said. "That leaves us few options."

Om grinned. "Smash and grab?"

I laughed. "Be afraid, we're starting to think alike."

"It's a rental," Om said.

"We used fake names," I added.

"GUN IT!" Om yelled.

"No," Al stated.

I slammed on the gas and accelerated straight into the window in the corner of the building, hoping nobody put any of the equipment against the outer wall. The vehicle smashed solidly into the building. Glass shattered, wood cracked, metal crunched. Before the dust settled, Al exited the car and plowed his way inside.

I backed the vehicle up, relieved it was still running. Om jumped out to help Al. I couldn't see much, but I could hear. The place erupted into complete chaos. Alarms were howling, and there was a lot of shouting. I looked at my watch. Two minutes had passed.

Then, I detected movement. There was some kind of shuffling in the dusty haze of the building. Then, there was more shouting. First, I heard Om, then Al. The next thing I knew, they were running toward the car. Security guards were giving chase.

"Drive!" Om yelled as they dived into the car. I pressed the accelerator. The vehicle jerked into motion. Gunshots fired behind us. The back window was shot out.

"Faster!" Om screamed. "There are rent-a-cops."

"Rent-a-cops with guns? Shit!" I screeched out of the parking lot and onto the local roads. The guards followed in a security vehicle. Lights and sirens screamed behind us. This was not going to be a quiet escape.

"We need to work on our stealth," I stated.

"You did not just say that," Om replied. "You."

"I said 'we'."

I weaved through side streets to lose them. "They'll stop. They have no real law enforcement power."

They kept up with us, however.

"You were saying?" Om asked.

"It appears this has become personal for them," Al stated.

"Just our luck," I complained. "We get the guys who take their jobs seriously."

I tried to go faster, but the vehicle had nothing else to give me.

"Shit," I cursed. "I don't want to hurt these guys."

"Since when?" Om asked.

"Since they didn't do anything to us and are only doing their legal fucking jobs."

"Oh," Om replied. "You do have a conscience."

I shook my head. "You think I would have saved you if I didn't? Shit, the only reason I went on Keen's magic ride was to watch you kids. I was ready to walk away after Keen started getting loose with his deadly force."

"You stayed for us?"

"Mostly you," I answered. "You still have the light in you."

"The light?" Om asked. "What light?"

"You know, the freaking light. Wanting to save the world and all that shit. Even through all the bullshit, you still have the light. That's worth saving."

"I… Thanks. I didn't know."

"You wouldn't," I replied. "I didn't tell you."

More gunshots were fired as the security guards started closing the distance.

"So, what do we do now?" I asked.

"Go faster," Al said. "And farther."

"You're so fucking helpful." I tried to get more power out of the car. It started smoking and sputtering. I took a sharp left down an alley at full speed. The security guards blew past, unable to turn in time. I took a right and another left and forced the angry vehicle forward.

I looked in the rearview mirror and didn't see anyone behind me. It appeared that I managed to shake the guards loose.

"Where now?" Om asked.

"As far as this bucket will take us," I answered. "So, not far enough."

"Aren't you some kind of electrical engineer?" Om asked. "Can't you at least try to fix this thing?"

"Yeah." I looked around for a quiet space to pull over, some place with enough light to see what I was doing. I found a spot tucked away in a parking lot that was bright enough but not out in the open. I didn't have much in the way of tools, so I did my best with what I had. The damage was severe, but I bypassed a few things to get us going. It wouldn't last long, but it was enough to get us away. I got back into the vehicle and started it. The smoking stopped, and it sounded much better.

"Maybe you should use your brain more often," Om said. "Instead of always using brute force."

"Maybe you should shut the fuck up," I replied.

"You both need to eat something," Al said. "You're tired and hungry."

"We need to get the hell out of here," I said. "Please tell me you got what we needed."

"I did," Al replied.

"Finally, something."

We sped off into the night, driving for hours until we didn't even know where we were. We pulled into a drive-through, grabbed chow, and got a room in a generic motel down the street from a strip mall. I dropped Al and Om off at the room and drove out of town to ditch the car. Taking advantage of the ten-kilometer walk back, I cleared my head, enjoying the cool evening air.

When I returned to the room, Al was sitting in a corner, and Om was still eating.

"About time," she said.

"Save me any food?" I asked.

She threw a bag at me. I caught it and sat at the table across from her.

"Chinese?" I asked. "I thought you got burgers. How is it still hot?"

"I just made a second run," she said. "I was really hungry."

"Cool." I tore into my food.

"How did we make out?" I asked Al. "Was it worth the bullshit?"

"It was worth the bullshit," Al replied. "I have information."

"Really?" I shoved half of an egg roll into my mouth. "What did you get?"

"Carnal Max, also known as the artist Max, was formally Maxwell W. Johnston, disgruntled ex-employee of Cretonic Real Estate."

"Mmm, no kidding," Om said through her mouthful of fries.

"What does he have on them?" I asked.

"Not just them," Al answered. "A whole consortium of realtors that cater to only the highest echelon of clientele. The conspiracy is real. Maxwell has the names and evidence of every top-level participant in the conspiracy. The paper trail is here."

"Stupid realtors!" Om cursed.

"Seriously?" I asked. "A real estate conspiracy? How is that even possible?"

"The evidence is compelling," Al replied.

"I suppose it's no different from any other price-fixing the banks have done in the past," I said. "What's the angle this time?"

"It's very simple," Al explained. "They intend to crash the real estate market, buy up everything for cheap, renovate, and sell at a huge profit to the ultra-rich. Then, they use the people they displaced as slave labor for their other enterprises. Legal confirmed that part."

"How are they getting away with this?" Om asked. "Aren't there regulations?"

"Yeah." I nodded. "Regulations are written by the politicians that the rich people put into office. I'm surprised they didn't do this shit sooner."

"This is bad," Om stated.

"Just like Boss Doom in Carnal Max." I sighed. "I'll definitely need therapy after this."

"It gets worse," Al continued.

"Let me guess, doomsday."

Al nodded. "The Hanul nuclear fission plant in Korea."

"What?" I snapped. "I was joking about doomsday. They don't even use nuclear fission anymore. It's too dangerous."

"It was reactivated over a year ago."

"Why?" Om asked.

"Let me guess," I said. "Some realtors bought it."

"Yes," Al answered. "Because they plan to melt it down."

Om stopped eating.

"Well, shit," I said. "This is a steaming pile. How will Nexum upsell irradiated real estate?"

"They also own the only company that holds a patent to clean up nuclear contamination."

"RidNuke, fuck." I shook my head. "But why did they reactivate me then?"

"I believe it was an accident," Al explained. "You were on the list of people to keep subdued. RoboBash must have thought he could take you out. He was probably looking to gain favor from the people in charge. His body was found in a dumpster three days ago. Working for Keen was probably Plan B — a way to keep you under surveillance and misdirect you."

"Wait, something doesn't make sense." I shook my head. "How would RoboBash find me? I had it locked down. Nobody knew where I was… except."

Al looked away. "I'm sorry."

"What did you do, Al?"

"I accidentally showed RoboBash where you lived."

This time, Om scoffed. "Holy crap, you sent that guy to kill your girlfriend?"

"No," Al answered. "I had set up a direct link to her house. Robobash stumbled upon it when he was looking for you."

I pointed at Al. "You were stalking me."

"I already told you that I was checking in on you from time to time."

"How would he find your feed?" Om asked. "Aren't you a master super hacker?"

"I was looking in on her at the same time that RoboBash was hunting her down. He caught a glimpse of my feed and found her."

"Shit. You knew I was coming back. That's why you weren't surprised. You knew the minute I died."

Al somehow managed to look dejected despite his lack of features. "Eris, I'm sorry. But at the same time, I'm not."

"Have you been feeling guilty about this the whole time?" Om asked.

Al nodded.

"You're an ass." I stood up and slapped Al in the head. It wasn't hard, but enough to know he had fucked up.

"I deserved that."

"Yes, you did," Om said.

"Well, aren't we a hot mess?" I sighed and squeezed Al's shoulder. "I forgive you. You're only human like the rest of us."

"I'm sorry," Al repeated.

"I know, aaibee. I know." I kissed him on the forehead. "This whole thing is a steaming pile, a real shit storm."

"A perfect shit storm," Om added. "With periods of torrential diarrhea."

"We need to put a stop to this," I said.

"Yes," Om said. "We will be the TP that plugs this mess."

"Ew," I replied. "So, what? Now we're the fiber that binds the shit together?"

Om giggled. "Go, team."

"Where do we fucking start? Al, do you have any ideas?"

"Nothing yet."

"Well, think about it." I yawned. "I'm getting some sleep."

I was tired. So, I slept all night and woke up at sunrise. Al was sitting in front of the window, watching. I got up and stood next to him.

I laid my hand on his shoulder. "How are you doing, aibee?"

He grabbed my hand. "Better now."

"You're sweet," I replied. "The girl sleep through the night?"

"Yes, she was exhausted."

"How are we going to stop this? How will we even get to Korea?"

"I'm working on that. I had to seek additional assistance. I've made sure the data is in safe hands. If we fail, someone will pick up where we left off."

"Yeah, who? Everyone but you and Om seems to be in it for the payoff."

"There are others," Al answered. "You don't go where they go."

"What? The bar? Because that's the only place I see you go. What amazing place do you go?"

Al laughed. "I never said it was amazing. I said *you* don't go there."

"But you are amazing."

"You have too much faith in me."

"You never failed me," I said. "Me, not so reliable."

"You're perfect."

I laughed. "You're wrong."

"No." Al shook his head.

"Yes, liar." I squeezed his shoulder. "But you meant virtual, didn't you?"

"I did. I know people who are good at dispersing information. They particularly like to take down what they consider to be overreaching organizations."

"Well, these assholes fit the bill. Your people will make sure they get busted?"

"They'll try."

"I never knew you were such an elite hacker. I should have figured it out a long time ago. Under that calm façade, you're a virtual warrior."

"I do what I need to. Part of my deal was to behave."

"Wait." I grinned. "Deal? Sounds like you're on parole. What exactly did you do?"

"I might have threatened death from above on a much larger scale. I needed to make a point."

"Oh, you are a badass. What exactly can you access?"

"A lot more than you would be comfortable knowing about."

"I'm comfortable with everything about you," I replied. "Even if you can doom us to the dark ages."

Al dropped his voice low to a whisper. "I can."

"Well, with all that power, you should be able to fly us to Korea with no problem."

Al laughed. "Are you sure you're okay?"

"With you?" I shrugged. "Yeah, why wouldn't I be? Remember, I'm Death Engine."

"That's not what I mean. You've been dragged out of your home, repeatedly killed, and viciously tortured. You hold it inside and act like it doesn't affect you. But I know it does."

"Of course it does," I replied. "But I was trained for this."

Al shook his head. "No, you weren't trained for this. This far exceeds what any person should live through."

"I can't afford to think about it," I explained. "If I allow myself to ponder things too much, I'll fall apart."

"That's not healthy. You need to let it out."

"You sound like the girl. I'll tell you what, when this is all done, you, me, and our little girl can sit down and talk about our feelings as long as you want. Until then, we stay focused, strong, and do this thing."

"You're not expendable. You're not a tool. You're my soulmate."

"I, wow, I—"

"You don't have to say anything," he said. "Just take care of yourself for me."

I grinned. "How about you and me in the bathroom for a quickie before the girl wakes up?"

"There is no quickie with you. Besides, we must stay focused and strong until this is over."

"Touché. Well, in that case, I'll need food. I'm going to drown my sorrows in donuts and coffee. Be right back."

"Don't be long and bring something back for Onyx."

"You got it." I gave him a thumbs up.

Although I lost track of what town we were in, I found a convenience store in the strip mall. Unfortunately, the stock was nonexistent, and what was there had expired. So, I wandered until I found a supermarket a few blocks away. I started filling my cart with the essentials, coffee, junk food, and liquor. The expiration dates on the food were cutting it close, but still all right. As I perused the aisles, my only company was an elderly couple, apparently doing their routine shopping. They walked arm in arm, pushing their cart at a leisurely pace. The woman leaned her head on the man's shoulder and smiled.

"Really," I muttered. "Does it have to be so heavy-handed?"

"You're talking to yourself," the old man shouted down the aisle. "Come talk to us. We'd like the company."

"No." I turned around to face them. "I'm not talking to myself. I'm talking to the universe."

"You should try talking to people instead. You're more likely to get a response."

"Nah," I said. "The universe answers me. Just not the way I want."

"How long have you been alone?" the man asked.

"I'm not alone," I replied. "I have people. But I'm having a dispute with the universe."

"What did the universe do to you?" the woman asked.

I just laughed. The old lady's smile faded.

"Am I to assume you were not satisfied with the outcome?" the old man inquired.

"Outcome?" I asked. "There's no real outcome."

"When one door closes," the woman said. "Another opens."

The man nodded. "Whatever you think the universe did to you, there had to be a result, an outcome. Something happened, and there was an effect."

"The universe crapped on me repeatedly," I replied. "And it continues to do so."

"What exactly does it do to you?" the woman asked.

"Okay, let's do this," I replied. "It repeatedly dishes out excruciating physical pain and will not let me die."

"You want to die?" the woman asked. "Why would you want to die?"

"Because I'm tired," I answered. "Every time it hurts me, it makes me come back for more. It's too much."

The woman shook her head. "It can't be that bad."

"No? You're right. It's so much fun. I'm lucky that I lived through drowning more than once. And being set on fire. And shot, stabbed, beaten, and irradiated. Oh, and being thrown in acid was a real winner. Can't get enough of that. I especially loved falling to my death. The anticipation of the impact is golden. Then there's the torture. Ever had your tongue cut out? I just adored that. I'm not exaggerating this shit. It's fucking ridiculous. I'd had enough seventy years ago, and I've had enough now. But does it stop? No. Then, everyone around me nags me about needing therapy and sharing my feelings. I don't need therapy. I just need this bullshit to stop. I need to fucking die already. I'm tired of being the freaking Death Engine. I want to be done."

"But at least you have your health." The man grinned.

"Fuck me," I growled.

"Obviously, someone cares," the woman said. "Or they wouldn't nag you. Doesn't that mean anything to you?"

I threw my head back in frustration. "Yes, it means something. But is it really enough to keep fighting?"

"That's on you," the man said. "But obviously, the universe has a plan for you, and you've not finished it yet."

"The universe is a bitch," I replied. "But thank you. Thank you for letting me vent."

"It's okay," the woman said. "Everybody has their cross to bear. Yours is just very large."

I sighed and shook my head. I started pushing my cart away from them toward the checkout.

"I liked you better with pink hair," the man shouted.

"Of course you did."

Al found a charter airline that didn't ask any questions. Om, Al, and I piled into our new rental vehicle. It would be a half day's drive to the airport, and whatever time it would take to finalize our negotiations for the charter.

It was a scenic drive past familiar territory.

"Wait!" I shouted. "Turn left here."

Om took the turn. "Why?"

"I want to see Jack," I said.

"Is that wise?" Al asked.

"Fuck it, I want to see him."

"Who's Jack?" Om asked.

We drove into the back gate of Champion Acres. I still have the override code I coaxed out of maintenance years ago. We went through the palatial estates, where popular heroes of military, civil, and humanitarian fame resided. These were the headliners. The people who saved thousands and were known globally.

Then, we cruised past the more modest homes where regular heroic folks lived. These people put their lives on the line daily but never receive fame or fortune. They had small, tidy homes and peaceful lives that they had earned through their service to others. Their pride was in the lives they touched, not the pursuit of fame and wealth.

Then we hit my old neighborhood: the trailer park. These were populated by technically qualified people but were not so well regarded. A few operatives could not disclose their qualifications, ex-spouses of known heroes, and sidekicks of varying types. My neighbor, Dori, had seen some shit, but it was so classified she had nothing to put on her application. We'd sometimes talk in code about it.

"Pull up here," I said.

Om complied, and I jumped out of the vehicle, gazing at the yard from a distance. Dori was lounging in her yard with a drink. Jack was chasing bees in the garden.

"You're going to scare the normals," Dori yelled. "You better come on over."

I crossed the street and walked into her yard.

"Jack looks good."

"He was getting fat, so I switched his food," Dori explained.

"Bet he hated that."

"Nah, he's pretty tolerant of change," Dori said. "You should go say hello."

I shook my head. "I don't want to confuse him. I feel bad enough about abandoning him."

"Don't. Jack understands. He saw the whole thing. He told me."

"Let me guess," I replied. "Jack said 'meow'."

"Indeed." Dori grinned. "You know, all these years, I suspected it was you. I would've been a little less polite if I had been sure."

"I dropped enough hints. I wanted to tell you."

"There are things I still want to tell you, but Jack wouldn't like it if I did."

"Jack gets funny," I replied. "Always used to tell me to keep my mouth shut and pass the catnip."

"Yes," Dori agreed. "He does like his nip."

"Well, everyone knows about me now."

"You're the talk of the community," Dori stated. "They're going on about how we had the Death Engine here all along and didn't know it. You're something of a celebrity around these parts now."

"It's been a while since I had any positive press."

"Well, us elderly folks remember who you used to be."

I grinned. "Bet my talent show performance made a lot more sense now."

Dori nodded. "Nobody does a tripstep remake of 'Genie in a Bottle' like Captain Eris."

"Yeah."

"I see you gathered a crew already." Dori nodded in the direction of Om and Al.

"I got myself into some shit," I replied. "I needed the help."

"They seem committed," Dori stated. "They've been watching us the whole time."

"They're worried. Especially Al. He's been dragged into my crap for years."

"He's got the same immortality problem you have?"

"Not the same, but yes. He has a similar one."

"So, you have good company."

"Yes," I replied. "I do."

"You know, there aren't many in these parts that would have sympathy for your affliction."

"I know. I probably wouldn't either."

"So," Dori asked. "What's the action?"

"The action." I laughed. "Renegade realtors doing evil. They're trying to empty the planet and renovate it for the rich."

"Ah, that explains the push to relocate the community to Mars, well, most of it."

"Let me guess, this part would go to the Outer Colonies."

Dori nodded.

"Don't let them do it," I said. "It's a trap."

"I wasn't planning on it. Jack likes it here."

"Jack's a stubborn guy. He knows what he likes."

"Are you going to be alright?" Dori asked.

"I'll survive," I replied. "I always do."

"Surviving is fine, but there's more to life."

"I know. Maybe things have been getting a little better." I glanced over at the vehicle. "Good company hasn't hurt any."

"I can see it," Dori said. "Jack thinks you should come back and visit after you finish your business."

"I will."

"Promise? We'll grill."

"I promise."

"Good." Dori squeezed my shoulder with her frail but steady hand. "Fix this mess and come home."

I nodded and walked back to the vehicle. We all piled inside in silence.

"Jack's fine," I said. "He said we need to visit more often."

Al reached over the front seat and took my hand.

Chapter 11

We drove for several more hours until we arrived at the airport. Arriving a day and a half early for our meeting, we checked into a room to wait. After ordering a pizza, Om rented some pay-per-play games. I was impressed with her skill. After a while, she decided to get some rest, so she locked herself in the bathroom for a hot bath.

Al started compiling a checklist of things we might encounter on our trip and tried to prepare for them. His list was getting long and complicated.

"We'll need some guns," he stated.

"That's funny coming from you," I replied.

"I can't find any way around it."

"I could probably get some weapons, but I don't know how we'll get them on a plane, never mind through customs."

"Leave that to me," Al said. "You just get them."

"Okay, aibee. I'll hit one of my stashes and replenish the coin. I know a guy nearby."

"Take Onyx," Al said.

"You sure that's a good idea? We keep dragging her into the shit, but to see arms dealers? These guys are known douchebags."

"She can handle it," Al replied. "You need the backup."

"Fine, fuck it. Om!" I called into the bathroom. "Finish washing your ass. We have an errand to run."

"I was just getting comfortable," she whined.

"Oh, poor baby," I replied. "Al, our poor little merc-girl was getting comfortable, and I'm ruining it."

"That's a shame," Al said.

"Oh!" Om stomped out of the bathroom, wrapped in a towel. "You two suck."

"Stop your bitching," I said. "There's shit to do."

Om grumbled as she got dressed. I emptied the clothes from my overnight bag and took it with me. Om followed me to the vehicle, still visibly irritated. I drove to the nearest hardware store.

"Please go inside and buy a shovel. I need to dig a hole." I handed Om some cash. She grabbed it and stormed off. A few minutes later, she returned with the shovel. She threw it in the back seat.

"Thank you," I said as she sat in the passenger seat beside me.

"Bite me," she replied.

I laughed. "Okay, besides pulling you from your bath, what the fuck did I do?"

"You treat me like I'm a kid."

"You are a kid," I replied. "But you're our kid, so it's okay."

"I am not your child. You didn't give birth to me. And there is no way Al is my father."

"You've been adopted. Get used to it unless you really object."

"Just like that? Why?"

"We like you." I patted her on the knee. "Is it so bad? It's a step up from your crack whore mother, right?"

Om scoffed. "Can't you just treat me like an adult?"

"We do. We treat you like a less experienced adult. If we really treated you as a child, you wouldn't be on this trip."

Om sighed and threw herself back in the seat. "Okay, but just stop referring to me as 'the girl'."

"Maybe," I replied.

"You are *such* a bitch."

I shrugged. "I am what I am." I pulled the vehicle over to the side of the road near a wooded area. "Wait here. Honk if anyone stops." I jumped out and grabbed the shovel and bag. "Be right back."

The trees grew thick and undisturbed. A faded, crooked sign stood on the edge of the woods, advertising sixty acres of commercial space available. I counted myself extremely lucky for the lack of development. Pulling out my comm, I brought up the compass. The spot was about 2 kilometers in. Once I found the place, I started to dig, hoping it was still there. Fortunately, finding the metal box that held one of my emergency stashes didn't take long. I emptied the box into the bag and buried it where it had been. I returned to the vehicle to find Om looking nervous.

"You okay?" I asked as I threw the shovel and bag in the back seat.

"Yeah," Om said. "A bunch of trucks drove by. It was nerve-wracking. What's in the bag?"

"The severed head of my enemy," I replied.

Om rolled her eyes.

"What do you think?" I asked. "It's cash."

"How much coin?"

"Two hundred and fifty thousand," I replied.

"How many stashes do you have?"

"Enough," I replied. "You should start thinking about contingencies yourself. It's a good idea to have a 'get out of Dodge' plan."

"A what?" Om asked.

"A fucking escape plan. Listen, the place we're going to could be cool but could also be a shit storm. I need you to hang back and be prepared to call for backup."

"You mean call Al if you mess up."

"Oh, you're asking to be bitch-slapped."

"I'm only stating the obvious. There's a pattern."

I shook my head. "You know, I fucking help him, too."

"Yeah, but you're higher maintenance than him."

"So, now you're a daddy's girl?"

"Yeah." Om grinned. "Guess I am."

"I'll remember that."

We drove another hour before making it to our destination. It was a mechanic's shop out in the middle of nowhere. I pulled in close to the door if things went wrong, and I had to run. I got out of the vehicle and took the bag. "Wait here. You can get out, but don't go anywhere. Stay near the vehicle."

"Okay, Mom."

I grinned and went inside.

Just as I entered the door, a large man in a pair of coveralls stopped me. "Can I help you?"

"I'm here to see Tom Tom," I replied.

"Tom Tom is long gone," a man said from behind the counter. "Who the hell are you?"

"I'm Eris. We used to do business."

"Well, Tom Tom has been gone for years. I'm John. I run the place now. Tim."

A young man in his early twenties stepped out of an office. "Yeah, Pop."

"Go inside and get Grandad's book, please."

"Okay, Pop."

The boy went into the office and came out with a tattered-looking journal. John started flipping through the book. "Eris, hmmm, Eris." He flipped a few more pages and stopped. "Oh, hell."

Tim looked over his shoulder, and his jaw dropped. "Death Engine."

"No," John said.

"I never did Tom Tom wrong, why not?"

"It says here that you are a harbinger of doom. Every time you did business with him, pandemonium followed. Pandemonium. It's written right here. See that, Tim?"

"I see it there, Pop. It says pandemonium."

"It seems that people look for you," John said. "Angry people. People who make trouble. So, it's time for you to leave."

"I'm already here, so what does it matter?"

"Harbinger of doom," Tim said. "Pop just said."

"But I already walked in the door. So, doom would be coming anyway."

"But if you leave now, I can say I didn't do business with you. I believe I'm going to make that choice."

"I have cash," I replied.

"Everyone has cash," John said.

I threw my arms in the air. "Fucking great. Okay, I'm out." I scooped up my bag on the way to the exit.

"Wait, who's that?" Tim pointed out the front window at Om, leaning up against the vehicle.

"That's Om, I mean Onyx. Leave her alone. She isn't going to do anything."

"Is she your kid?" Tim asked.

"Kind of, in a weird, dysfunctional, non-blood related way."

"Tell her to come inside," Tim said.

"I don't think that's a good idea."

"Like Tim said, tell her to come in," John stated.

"Fine." I motioned Om to come inside. She obliged.

"Now you get out," John said. The large man by the door leveled a weapon at me.

"That doesn't work, you know."

"Get out," John repeated.

"Don't you harm her, or I will fucking teach you about pandemonium firsthand." I handed Om the bag. "Even if they offer you the whole inventory, not a penny over one hundred thousand."

I stepped outside and waited by the car.

I watched through the window. At first, Om and Tim were just talking. It seemed calm. Then Tim grabbed an empty beer can and crushed it against his forehead. Om grabbed another can and crushed it against her own forehead. Then she took the cinder block they used as a doorstop and smashed it over her skull. Tim seemed very impressed.

Next, I saw Om and Tim arm-wrestling on either side of the counter. Om had to stand on a step stool to reach it, but that didn't stop her. It only took moments for her to defeat Tim. Once again, he seemed impressed.

They spoke for a bit longer, and then Tim disappeared into the back. Om came out with the bag a few minutes later, and Tim appeared from around the back carrying an armful of firearms. Om opened the trunk, and Tim put the weapons inside. She closed the trunk and shook Tim's hand.

"It was a pleasure doing business with you," she said.

"Yes," Tim replied. "Please come see us again. Just don't bring her."

"You got it," Om said.

She got in the passenger seat, and I sat behind the wheel. I drove off before they could change their minds.

"How much did you have to pay?"

"Twenty-five thousand," Om answered.

"That trunk full of plasma weapons for twenty-five thousand. Did you blow Tim when I wasn't looking?"

Om sneered. "I blew nobody. Tim bet me that he could beat me arm wrestling. I'd pay half if I won, double if I lost."

"You know that is a terrible bet," I said. "You took the higher risk."

"Only if I lost, which I did not. You said nothing over one hundred thousand."

"Fine," I replied. "How did this freaking bet even come about?"

"When I walked in, Tim wanted to know why 'such a pretty little thing was hanging out with that monster.' I told him I was hella tough. And it started from there."

"Why am I always the monster?"

"Maybe people say monster but mean bitch."

"So what, you're friends with Tim now?" I asked.

"Guess so," Om answered. "I make friends a lot easier than you."

"You're never going to let this go, are you?"

"Nope." Om grinned. "Time for you to call and check in."

"Why don't you just do it? You can gloat and get it over with."

Om picked up her comm and called Al.

"Are you safe?" he asked.

"We're fine," Om replied. "We're on our way back."

"Good. Keep in touch if anything changes." Al closed the call.

"What? No gloating?" I asked.

"I'll wait until we get back."

"Great."

The trip back to the motel was uneventful. We moved the weapons under the cover of darkness and motel blankets in case someone checked out the car. We stashed them in one of the dressers. It's not really safe, but it's out of obvious sight.

Om returned to her bath. I tried to nap but couldn't get comfortable.

"I'm going to the convenience store to pick up a six-pack."

"You shouldn't step outside," Al said. "Our other stops may have attracted unwanted attention."

"I need the air," I replied. "And a drink. It's just across the street. Be right back."

"Be careful."

"Yeah," I replied as I closed the door behind me. I walked directly to the store and grabbed a six-pack and some beef jerky. I paid and stepped outside.

"Well, there she is," a familiar voice called from behind me.

"Oh, hell," I muttered to myself. "Fuckwad! You old shitbag, what brings you to this lovely suburban paradise."

"Why you do, my beautiful robot wanker."

"Technically, that would be robot fucker."

"I stand corrected. Where is it?"

"Where is what?"

"Don't act coy with me, Eris. You know exactly what I'm talking about. I spotted you at the Acres. What kind of idiot stops to visit their cat when they know they're being hunted?"

"Go fuck yourself."

"You always were a crude bitch."

I shook my head. "People say that as if it was a bad thing."

Keen pulled out a sword. It was engraved with designs and was very shiny.

"Nice magic sword," I noted.

"Oh, this sword? It was given to me by an expert sword maker. It was painstakingly crafted for one sole purpose."

"To look shiny and pretty?"

"No," the fuckwad replied. "To remove problems like you. But you know what makes it special?"

"It's sharp and pointy?"

"You know your problem? You don't appreciate the finer things. You have no taste."

"Untrue," I replied. "I have taste. I'm just not a pretentious prick like you."

"Heh." Keen grinned. "Your mouth isn't getting you out of trouble this time. You know, you could never fight. You're a one-trick pony, relying on your tweak to get you out of everything. The trick is not letting you die."

"You've really thought this out," I stated.

"Yes, I have. See, this is how it's going to go down. I'm going to slice you up to the point that you can't move. All you'll be able to do is slowly bleed out. Then I'll leave you here and go kill the kid. And after that, I'm going to track down your boyfriend and power him down."

"You can try, but maybe we want to move away from this high-traffic area so we don't hurt any civilians."

"Since when have you cared about collateral damage, Death Engine?"

"See, you just can't stop bringing that up."

Keen laughed. "You're going down this time, you infernal cunt."

"Whoa, language," I said.

Fuckwagen swung his magic sword and sliced me across the chest.

"Ow," I complained. "That hurt."

"Oh, it's going to hurt a lot more, sweetheart."

He swung again, clipping me in the arm. I took the opportunity to throw a punch. I missed.

"Tsk, tsk, you telegraph too much. You never studied."

I tried to kick him but failed. He effortlessly carved open my leg. It was bleeding badly.

"Look, you're completely off balance," Keen pointed out. "It's embarrassing."

He was correct. I was a shitty fighter, but that wouldn't stop me. I took another swing, which he easily dodged and cut me in the shoulder.

"This is getting very annoying," I stated.

"Then maybe I should end it." Fuckmeister did some kind of leg sweep, and I stumbled backward into the store's wall. He held the point of the sword to my neck.

"I know you're just hoping I do it," he said. "Slice you open so you can come back diamond coated."

"Actually, that would be metallic. Diamond coating is blunt trauma and gunshots."

"My mistake," Keen sneered. "I'm going to cut you…"

The convenience store doorbells chimed as two teenage boys holding sodas stepped out. The door bumped Keen in the arm, causing him to fumble the sword and slice my throat.

I died. The trip to paradise was quick. The universe must have known I had shit to do.

I convulsed for a moment and then came back. When I got up, the boys were staring at me awkwardly.

"Where's the douchebag with the sword?" I asked.

They both pointed in Keen's direction. I saw him running several blocks away.

"You got a vehicle of some kind I can borrow?"

One of the boys handed me his electric scooter, and I gave him a wad of cash coins and took off after Fuckgasm.

Keen could run. But I had electricity behind me. It wasn't long before I caught up. I rammed the scooter right into him. He fell to the ground, and I landed on top of him. I began pounding on his face with my fist. He pulled out his sword and sliced at me, but it did nothing. I grabbed it by the blade, flipped it over, and stabbed Keen in the chest.

"Too late, you bitch," he gurgled. Then he died.

"Too late for what?" I muttered.

I left him there, magic sword and all, and walked the scooter back to the boys.

"Sorry, I scratched it a little. The coins should help you fix it."

"Wow," one of the boys said. "You kick ass."

"I'm a fine example of what hard living and mental illness can achieve. You boys have a nice day."

That's when I heard the gunshots.

I ran back to the room and found the door wide open. A large man was embedded into the far wall. He had a 'ReJects Real Estate' shirt on.

"Realtors," I muttered.

Another man was folded over the small corner table. Bullet holes blanketed the wall behind the bed, a hatchet was hanging from the ceiling, and the environmental system was crushed and smoking. Om was unconscious and bleeding from a wound on her forehead, but she was breathing. I checked her for injuries and found nothing life-threatening. I left her to find Al.

He was in the bathroom, his body sprawled across the tub. Someone had rammed the shower rod through his body and pinned him to the wall.

"Holy shit!" I yelled.

"I'm fine," he replied. "Is Onyx okay?"

"Out cold, but I think she's alright. How are you okay?"

"They didn't hit anything major," Al explained. "And the rod is nonconductive. It looks worse than it is."

I grabbed the end of the rod. "Okay, I am going to pull it out now. Brace yourself."

"Go ahead."

I pulled, and it came out smoothly. Al stood up. His shirt was torn, and I could see some chipped paint through the hole but not any sparking or overt sign of damage. I lifted his shirt and did a quick visual inspection.

He grabbed my hand. "I'm fine."

I shook my head. "Told you. Can't fight. You're a lover, not a fighter."

"I'm not having this argument again," Al said.

"Because you know I'm right."

"No," Al stated.

"They didn't damage any sensors, did they?"

He laughed. "Everything's intact."

"Ow!" Om yelled from the room. "My head is pounding."

I ran out and helped her up. "Who did this?"

"A bunch of realtor jerks," Om replied.

I nodded. "I saw the shirt."

"They were looking for the crystal drive," Al said

"Did they get it?" I asked.

"They got an incomplete copy," Al answered. "I was in the middle of backing up the data when they arrived."

"Why are you shiny?" Om asked. "Did they get you first?"

"Ding dong, the douchebag is dead." I grinned.

"Douchebag? You killed Keen?" Om's eyes got big. "How?"

"My superior skills and training, of course."

"Not likely," Al said.

"Okay, he died of sheer luck and irony, but we really need to go."

After loading the weapons in the trunk, we piled in the vehicle and took off. We drove a few kilometers until we were out of town.

"Al?" I asked. "Can you transmit the data to Legal while we drive? Or do we need to be still?"

"As long as I have a clear path to the sky, we should be fine."

"Okay, send him what you have while we can."

Al sat quietly for a few minutes.

"Hey there!" Legal's voice filled the vehicle. The sound of gunfire was audible in the background.

"We can provide you further information," Al said. "Are you ready to receive?"

"Send it on over!" Legal answered.

"Transmitting, now," Al said.

A moment later, Legal grinned. "Got it! Wow, this is some good stuff. Did you three get this yourselves?"

"Yes, we did," Om replied.

"You're a formidable team."

"I know," Al said.

"When this is over, we'll get together and catch up." Legal said. "Boy sends his love."

"Send him mine," Al replied. "Talk to you soon."

"Legal out."

"Glad that is done." I sighed. "Can you help Om scan for trouble?"

"Yes. Wait." Al looked out the back window. "Uh oh."

"Did you just say, 'uh oh'? Uh oh, what?"

"They're here," Al said.

"Who's here?" Om asked.

"Everyone," Al replied.

Om looked out the back window. "I don't see anything?"

I slammed on the brakes. The road was blocked beyond any hope of escape. Vehicles appeared out of nowhere to block us from behind.

"The realtors?" Om asked.

"Those are no realtors," I said. The road was swarming with government agent types, backed up by armed military personnel.

"No, they're not," Al said.

"How did they find us?" I asked. Then, I answered my own question. "Death from above."

"Death from above," Al agreed.

"Death from above?" Om asked. "What do you mean?"

"They traced us," I explained.

"No," Al corrected me. "They traced me."

"What do we do?" Om asked.

"I'll go talk to them," I replied.

Al grabbed my arm. "Be careful."

"Never." I grinned.

I stepped out of the vehicle with my arms over my head.

"It was all me, all my fault."

Two soldiers ran up, threw me to the ground, and cuffed me. I didn't resist.

They dragged me to my feet and over to the woman who seemed to be in charge.

"You crashed our expensive communications satellite into a major highway?" she asked.

"Yes, I crashed your junk."

"How did you do it? How did you infiltrate our systems? How did you control the telemetry?"

"I hacked the crap out of it."

"No," she replied. "You don't have the skill set to do this."

"I have a masters in electrical engineering."

"Where's the AI?"

"You can't have him."

"He gave us certain assurances," she said. "He broke our agreement."

"Maybe you should have handled your realtor problem, and this never would've happened."

"Realtor problem?"

"What?" I asked. "You don't know?"

"I know that you are in big trouble here, Captain."

"Wait now, I'm not a captain anymore. You people let me go. Remember the lab and the dead people?"

"Technically, we never did anything about your commission."

"Well then, you owe me some serious back pay."

"What exactly is the nature of your relationship with artificial intelligence 1A-1?"

"I don't know anyone by that name," I replied.

"Stop playing games, Captain."

"Again with the captain shit. Listen, you have a problem. It crapped in my universe, and now you're trying to bully me into whatever irrelevant, bureaucratic hell you have in mind. I'm not biting. So, either fucking arrest me or cut me loose so I can deal with this shit and go home."

"I have no idea what you're talking about," she said.

"No shit. You have no idea about anything."

"Why did the AI crash my satellite?"

"Because," I answered. "A bunch of megalomaniac real estate agents sent an army of tweaks after us, and it was the only way we could survive."

"That is the most ridiculous thing I've ever heard."

"Oh, so you didn't find any bodies or evidence supporting my story at the crash site?"

"Tell the AI and the girl to come out."

"Guarantee their complete safety and freedom, and I will."

"I can guarantee their safety, but the AI will see prison time."

"You will not reacquire Al," I stated. "I'll bring a hell of chaos and death upon you for generations if you even try."

"We have the means to stop you."

"Oh, do you? Are you sure?"

She glared at me for a while, no doubt wondering if I would really back up my threats. An underling ran up and whispered something in her ear. She picked up her comm unit and stepped away. I watched her from a distance, having what appeared to be a very heated conversation with someone over the comm. Finally, she returned.

"Okay," she said. "We may be able to arrange something."

"Yeah, let me guess. You have a situation, and you need us. If we help you this one small time, we can go, but you're going to keep an eye on us. We better not step even a fraction out of line. Blah blah blah."

"We do have a situation," she said.

"The reactor."

"You know?" she asked.

"Well, yeah, the fucking realtors did it."

"Soldier, cut her loose. Captain, let's talk."

"How about you join me in my lovely budget rental for some conversation and cold comfort food? Just don't look in the trunk."

"Lovely."

I led her inside and sat next to her in the back seat. Al took the driver's seat.

"Good afternoon," she said. "I am Senior Agent in Charge, Brown."

"Hello, Brown," Om replied.

I laughed.

"You must be Cherry Petra."

"Cherry?" I asked. "Oh my sweet fucking lord, your mother named you Cherry."

Om looked humiliated. "Yes," she answered. "My mother was a crack whore. What else would she name me?"

"That is like the ultimate stripper name," I replied.

"That's why I don't give a crap that you call me Om."

"Ah, makes more sense now."

"Are we done?" Brown asked.

"These agent types ask us that a lot," Om said.

"Yup."

Brown must have decided she had enough of us and turned her attention to Al.

"You must be artificial intelligence 1A-1."

"His name is Al, Senior Agent in Charge, shithead."

"Okay, Al," she continued. "You crashed my satellite into a public highway. Why was that?"

"I was out of options. The satellite was classified as inoperable. An army of renegade, enhanced humans were about to capture and harm my girlfriend and our friend, so I made a choice."

"Your girlfriend?"

"Yes," he replied.

"What?" I asked. "You have regulations against that now."

Brown turned her attention back to me. "You know it's not alive."

"No, I know you are a fuckbag, whore, shitstain, racist."

"Wow," Brown responded. "You have feelings for this thing."

"Call him a thing one more time, and I will fuck you up so hard, you will shit your teeth for the next week."

"Al, you do understand that to have a girlfriend, you have to have emotions."

"I have emotions," he answered. "Do you?"

"What is your point, agent hag face?" I asked. "Because I'm losing my patience and any desire to cooperate."

"Yeah," Om added.

"Okay, my point. The Hanul nuclear power is melting down, and we can't get anyone or anything in there to stop it. We can't send any personnel in without certain death, and we keep losing drones. The environmental damage will be irreversible if we don't control this very soon. Our only option is you."

"What about RidNuke?" I asked.

"How did…" Brown paused. "They aren't cooperating. It will take months of litigation to force their assistance."

"Not if you have proof they are involved in the conspiracy," I replied.

"Do you have this proof?" Brown asked.

Al held up the crystal drive.

"We do this, and you do what it takes to make our lives harassment-free. Do you understand?"

"Captain, if you can just stop this meltdown, we will make sure the three of you live very comfortably."

"And free," I added.

"And free."

"Okay, let's go."

—⋀⋀⋀—

Our chopper landed about twenty kilometers away from the power plant. It was considered dangerously close but safe enough for short-term exposure. The place more resembled something owned by the military than a power company. We were escorted to a tent that was set up as central control. Armed guards manned the perimeter as if it were some kind of classified facility. When I entered the tent, I saw why.

It was filled with computers and racks of equipment I couldn't begin to identify. Two large stands were propped up in a corner of the tent. The meanest, nastiest mech suit I'd ever seen was on the stand. Every millimeter of it was covered in weaponry of some kind. I nudged Om with my elbow.

"Someone should tell them that you can't defeat radiation with guns," I whispered.

"I wouldn't want to go up against that thing," Om giggled.

"I kind of want to wear it. Bet it would be a rush."

"You're pretty twisted," Om said.

"Yup."

We were guided to a plastic fold-up table with multiple tablets and varying graphics and tables. People sat around it like a makeshift conference room table. We joined them and sat.

A uniformed man approached us.

"Who's the girl?" he asked as he took his seat. "I only asked for the robot and the tweak."

"She was with them, Colonel," Brown replied. "The robot wouldn't leave her behind."

"Fine." He turned his attention to me and Al. "Which of you is going in? I'm assuming artificial intelligence 1A-1."

"Me," I replied. "Why would Al go in?"

He ignored me and addressed Al. "We made adjustments to your old body. It's been hardened to withstand the radiation. You could jump into it and take care of business."

"His old body?" I asked. "That walking death platform in the corner was your body?"

Om smirked. "Still want—"

I help up my hand. "Not the time."

Brown continued, "Al, it's an upgrade from what you have. It's far beyond the current state-of-the-art. You could keep it when you complete the mission."

"No," I snapped. "You can't seriously be considering this."

"You could die," Al stated. "I'll survive."

"They'll never let you go. It's a trap. Don't fall for it. You are *not* that thing."

"Not anymore, but I was. I told you I could fight."

"Fuck you! Not funny. I'll just pop into the reactor, die a little, and pop right back out."

"I can't let you do it," he said. "The prolonged radiation will kill you."

"We have no guarantees that you'll fare any better. Radiation screws with electronics, too."

"I stand a better chance," Al replied. "And I can backup."

"A backup that they'll control."

"I won't let you die," Al insisted.

"I like the person you are now. I'm not going to be the reason you become a monster. You're a far better human being than I am. Don't let them turn you into me."

"I don't care which of you goes in at this point," the colonel stated. "But it has to be soon."

"If you can harden the body, why don't you send in a drone?" I asked.

"Connectivity," Brown said. "They survive, but we can't see or control them."

"So, pre-program them and then send them in."

"That's too complex," Brown answered. "Too many variables."

"How long will it take to get Al plugged into the new body?" I inquired.

"An hour," Brown answered. "Maybe two."

"How long to deploy me?"

"Just the time it takes for you to get inside."

"There's your answer," I said. "I go."

Al slammed his fist on the table, and it cracked.

"No! You'll die." He got up and stepped into the empty stand beside the waiting body. "Do it."

"Fuck that!" I picked up a chair and started smashing equipment. "You're not destroying him!" I knew if I broke enough crap, they wouldn't be able to transfer Al. I didn't know what any of the hardware actually did, but I had an idea of what was important. Sparks started flying, and people were yelling. Someone tried to grab me, but it was too late. Then there was gunfire, and I was on the ground.

There I was on the beach. I sat up and noticed I was all alone.

"Is anyone here?" I yelled. "Hello?"

I got no reply. So, I started looking for the light. It took a moment to find it, but I dove straight in when I did.

Once the seizing was done, I opened my eyes. Pandemonium. More shouting.

"It will take hours to get the backup equipment from the beta site," Brown complained.

"Do it," the colonel replied. "And clean up this mess."

I stood up.

"I'm ready to go now," I said.

Al stepped over to me. His lack of facial expressions did not disguise his anger.

"I couldn't let you do it," I explained. "I need you the way you are."

"I'm very upset," he replied. "Do it fast, or I'm coming in after you."

"Captain," the colonel said. "You just destroyed millions in equipment with your emotional outburst."

"Fuck it, Sir. Dock my pay."

I was handed an NBC suit. I quickly dressed and let the technicians check me over. The suit would delay the onset of radiation sickness long enough to carry everything I needed with me. I would die inside the facility instead of out in the parking lot or driving to the site.

As planned, I drove over in a hardened vehicle. The place was barren. I could see where people had dropped what they were doing to run. Tools were strewn haphazardly—bicycles were left on the side of the road, and personal items were abandoned. It was unnerving.

I made it inside without incident. The facility was no longer secure. Alarms flashed, and sirens wailed. I followed the maps to navigate to my destination. I made it to the staff cafeteria before I started getting dizzy. I sat in one of the chairs and tried to call out, but I only received static on my comm. I sent out a message anyway, just in case. Deciding I would die there, I sat by the vending machines. Once I returned from death, I would have a quick snack and take care of business.

After sitting for a couple of minutes, I noticed a lump in my pocket. It was the sensor stimulator I had engineered just days ago. I patted it through my pants. I looked forward to deploying it on Al.

A few minutes passed, and I realized nothing was happening. Screw it. I got up and headed for the control room. I'd have to die en route. That's when I realized my error.

A safety sign was hung by the cafeteria door. It listed the radiation sickness symptoms, detailing the length of time until their manifestation. It also advised that with a hefty dose of radiation, despite the immediate onset of symptoms, death could follow within a period of two days to two weeks.

"Shit," I cursed. I would have to work through whatever symptoms I presented with.

I didn't have to wait long. Halfway to the control room, weakness set in. I stumbled to the floor, dropping my utility bag. Unable to stand, I tried to crawl. I dragged myself and my tool case down the hall, forcing my failing muscles to move. The world was spinning to the point that I lost all sense of direction. Still, I crawled onward, hoping I wasn't going in circles.

Next, I was struck by a wave of nausea. I retched inside the suit, covering my field of vision in vomit. In a panic, I scrambled to free my head. I tore at the suit until I got loose. My hair clung to the helmet and fell out in the process. I continued to puke until nothing remained in my stomach. I stayed there dry heaving for a while until I found myself too weak to continue.

I lay on the floor, compelling my mind to remain on target. My disorganized thoughts tried to congeal on my purpose, fumbling on past memories of previous operations. I recalled my days with the Peace League, fighting for the dream. All the planning and rescue operations were worthwhile. I didn't even mind the exploitation so much. Making the team music video had been a laugh.

Maybe I should have drawn the line with Nevin. Possibly, it would have been okay if I had. I could have lived and died a normal person and never even known that I was the Death Engine. Then again, I would have never met Al. Al.

Shaking and still nauseous, I forced myself back to my knees and proceeded to creep down the hallway again. That's when the diarrhea started. I paused every ten meters or so to crap and vomit blood, but I kept moving, leaving a trail of puke, shit, ichor, and hair behind me.

I reached the control room and pulled myself into a rolling chair. Grabbing the documentation, I spread it across the control panel. It was hard to focus. Chills and aching crept up on me. I could tell that I was running a high fever.

I wanted to rest. Exhaustion was overtaking me. I lifted my shirt to cool myself. A strong shock of cold shot through my body. It reminded me of the floor of Spaz's bathroom, my first time there. Most people knew that floor because they were too drunk to stand. I was there because my sketchy-ass employer wanted to dispose of me. He stabbed me in the entrance of the bar. I barely made it to the bathroom before croaking. Al found me and tried to save my life. That was the day we first became friends. Al. I had to get moving before he came after me.

It took several rereads of the technical docs before I could fully comprehend it. Shivering violently, I began dropping the control rods in place and venting the steam. I watched the instrument clusters. The temperatures were approaching normal, but not fast enough. It would be hours before they decreased sufficiently to declare it a success.

I could barely sit up. My head was pounding furiously. I slumped in the chair, wishing for a faster death. It wasn't coming. There was only wave after wave of debilitating pain. I started to pass out. Slapping myself in the face to stay awake didn't work. I considered rolling myself to the cafeteria to look for coffee. Still, I couldn't even fathom making that long roll down the hall.

I rechecked the readings. The temperature was still slowly dropping. I hoped the team would detect it off-site and Al would remain at his safe distance. Trying to psych myself through the suffering, I forced myself to imagine my life in another week. I visualized being tucked safely in our bed and pictured myself sipping coffee and complaining about getting up. My eyes closed, and I drifted off.

I dreamed about Al and Om. I saw myself drinking at the bar, enjoying a liquid that tasted like oranges. Om ate a pile of French fries and Al scolded me for not eating. It was good to be home.

"Al," I muttered. I felt his arms around me, lifting me and shielding me from the pain. "I'm sorry."

I forced my eyes open. My head was still throbbing. I was thirsty and achy. I was also no longer in the chair. Gazing up, I saw a mat black, intimidating form. It clutched me in its unfamiliar, weaponized arms, carrying me out of the control room and down the hall.

"Al," I moaned. "Why?"

He didn't answer.

The world continued to spin around me until I found myself in darkness.

I regained consciousness in a hospital bed. Sensors and needles covered my entire body. I could hear people whispering from across the room and the audio of the news feeds in the background.

"She's awake." I heard someone say. The sound of people shuffling in followed.

"She doesn't have long," the voice said. "Make your peace."

"There is no peace to be made," Al's unmistakable voice said.

"Al," I gasped.

"I'm here." He sat next to the bed and held my hand. "You're a freaking mess."

"You gonna paint me?" I coughed.

He squeezed my hand.

"How? I saw you inside."

"I used the body as a drone. I took your advice and pre-programmed it. I put a small copy of myself inside. The drone's sole purpose was to save you."

"You're amazing. You saved my ass again."

"Not fast enough," Al lamented.

"There's no reason for the drama. I'll be up soon enough."

"You don't know that," he said. "This is different."

"Al, I died from every fucking thing. I come back."

"That wasn't radiation."

"I died from radiation twice," I said.

"Those were quick, controlled, intentionally fatal doses, not prolonged exposure. The doctors are concerned about irreversible genetic damage."

"You worry too much."

"What if you die? What if you don't come back to me?"

"Then you go on. You remember me, and you go on." I smiled. "But I'm coming back. So, stop losing your shit."

I glanced up and noticed the vid screen on the wall. I was surprisingly relieved to see Brad and Lucy on the air. We mustn't have done that much damage to the station after all. Live footage showed authorities hauling in real estate agents. One shot showed Domineer in cuffs being escorted into a police vehicle.

"Did we win?"

"It appears we did," Al answered. "They caught most of the perpetrators and prevented any further ecological damage. They should be able to clean the radiation up within the month."

"How about Legal and Boy?" I asked.

"They've already begun the proceedings to recover the victims' properties."

"Fuck, yeah!" I coughed.

The doctor walked over and checked my vitals.

"How long until I reset?" I asked.

"If by reset you mean die, not long."

"Am I on any pain meds?" I asked.

The doctor nodded. "Several."

"You need to take me off them, or I may come back a little crazy. Can you turn them off now?"

"You'll be in considerable pain."

"That's okay," I replied. "Pain is no big deal."

The doctor turned off the drip. The discomfort hit me quickly. I winced in response.

"Fuck!" I cursed. "That was more than I expected."

"The doctor warned you," Al stated, still at my side.

"Shit, this is a fucked up way to die. Quick is much better. Can't you just distract the doctors and leave me a gun?"

"That's no longer an option," Al responded. "You're still hardened from when you got yourself shot in the staging area."

"Crap, shitty planning. How's Om?"

"She's fine. She's waiting outside. Would you like to see her?"

"Why the hell not?"

One of the staff called Om into the room.

"You look like crap," she said.

"And I feel even shitier. They're all acting like I'm dying or something."

"They're afraid the radiation has damaged you beyond the point of regeneration," Om explained.

"I know. It's bullshit. But just in case, promise you'll take care of this dweeb. He shouldn't be alone."

"You know I will," Om answered.

"Perfect." I got hit with a wave of agony. I gritted my teeth to avoid screaming. "So, aibee, you think we have time for a quickie."

Al stroked my cheek. "We could try. But I don't think the bed could take the weight."

"They should have bought Martian-made. Maybe if I get on top."

"Gross," Om complained.

"You're just jealous." The pain struck again, causing me to tense up. "You two don't have to stay for this."

"Yes, we do." Om grabbed a chair, sat on the other side of the bed and took my other hand.

"I'm used to doing this alone. I hate dragging you into the shit."

"We've both seen it," Al replied.

"That's right," Om forced a smile. "Captain Fucktastic."

I laughed. "You finally got one." A strong pang shot through my core. "Damn it!" I screamed. The staff shuffled around us, but I felt Al and Om still with me.

"Why is she off the pain meds?" one of the staff asked.

"Her own request," someone answered.

"Crazy bitch. Close the door so the other patients don't hear."

Another wave of pain hit, and I screamed again. It continued to intensify until suddenly, it was gone. The world began to fade away, slowly drifting into the distance. And then I was back at my beach.

This time, I had a choice.

I lay peacefully in the sand. The light shone to my left, inviting me to reanimation but not yanking me in like before. It called me back to the land of the living, the place of pain and movement, the home that had injured me for so many decades.

To the right, I could see a warm, inviting, open view of the cosmos. It beckoned with a calm that I'd never felt before.

"You've earned a rest," Death said. This time, he was well-dressed in a dark suit and tie. The universe hovered above us, smiling.

"Hell, yes," I replied. "I'm so tired. Freaking tired."

I saved the fucking world again, and Al was finally safe. My job was done. Om would keep the bastard in line and make sure he didn't make some boneheaded move to compromise himself. Oddly enough, I trusted her. She'd turned out to be quite the little badass. Yeah, they'd probably mourn the hell out of me. But they'd get over it and move on.

I looked at the cosmos, whirling and dancing, its beauty beckoning me to learn its secrets. I could see life, all existence, growing within every particle. Everything made complete sense. A feeling of utter peace washed over me. I reached out to touch it.

I was ready, ready to let go and take my final rest. I could join with the universe, be everywhere, meld with everything, and be free. Finally, the pain would end forever. I stood up and brushed the sand off my body.

"Thank you," I said to death. "Thank you," I said to the universe.

Just as I was about to depart to the great fucking beyond, I caught a glimpse of something black and electronic-looking in the sand. I reached down and pulled up Al's sensor stimulator.

I smiled as I gazed upon its perfection. My handiwork—non-violent and functional. Although the first test worked, I never got the chance to give it a thorough shakedown. Now, I'd never know for sure.

After taking one final inventory of my options, I stuffed the stimulator in my pocket. Then, I turned my back on the cosmos and its promise of a final rest. I rejected it all and walked back into the light, back home.

THE END

About the Author

Margret A. Treiber is a versatile writer celebrated for her work in speculative fiction and humor. She is the author of *Japanese Robots Love to Dance*, which recently won **First Place in The BookFest Awards 2025** for Science Fiction-Humor, Science Fiction-Robots, Computers, and AI. Her writing has also been featured in various publications, and she serves as the editor-in-chief of the speculative humor magazine *Sci-Fi Lampoon*. Beyond her literary pursuits, Margret works in technology and enjoys watching her birds' antics, often creating challenges for her spouse to tackle.

Her unique blend of humor and speculative fiction has garnered her a devoted following. In the expansive multiverse, Margret is a formidable force of good, evil, and everything in between—a true mixed bag. One persona, the alien demi-god Margret, single-handedly defeated the viral hibachi army of Monatchi Seven before collaborating with the Mushwreck Squad to combat the Higgsinator matter-reprogrammer force.

As Cyborg Margret, she saved an entire solar system by channeling a supernova through her power banks, sacrificing her physical form for the survival of trillions. Her consciousness now resides in a trailer park icemaker in Pago Pago, where thousands visit annually to receive sacred Margret ice and hope for her wisdom. Known as Margret the Planet Wrecker, she commands two-thirds of the galaxy, demanding total loyalty from her subjects. Parents reportedly use her name to scare unruly children into obedience.

Meanwhile, back on Earth, Margret resides with her wife, eagerly anticipating a future alien invasion collaboration. As the keeper of the unified theory, she humorously offers it for sale to the highest bidder—serious inquiries only.

www.ingramcontent.com/pod-product-compliance
Lightning Source LLC
Chambersburg PA
CBHW071234260626
47161CB00003BA/949